The NEBADOR series:

Book One: The Test

Book Two: Journey

Book Three: Selection

Book Four: Flight Training

Book Five: Back to the Stars

Book Six: Star Station

Book Seven: The Local Universe

Book Eight: Witness

Book Nine: A Cry for Help

Book Ten: Stories from Sonmatia

Also by J. Z. Colby:

Standing on Your Own Two Feet:
Young Adults Surviving 2012 and Beyond

Stories from Sonmatia

an epic young-adult science fiction adventure

includes the new novella:
Escape from Sonmatia Two
by J. Z. Colby

ten previously-published short stories,
the narrative about King Zolko's people on Sonmatia Four,
and three new short stories:

Still Voices
by Mary Anne Brenner

Floating Away
by Tiffany Pertranovich

The Lonely Space Dragon
by Sammy McNeil

Nebador Archives

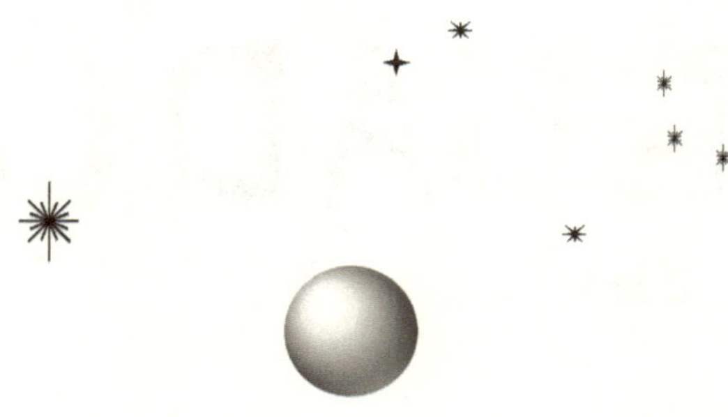

Copyright © 2016 by J. Z. Colby
All rights reserved

Cover art by Sidney Oster

Back cover art (from *NEBADOR Books One - Eight*)
    by Rachael Hedges, 1946-2015

For other print editions, ebooks, dramatic audiobooks, previews, samples,
biographies, comments, questions, artwork, writing contests, Ask Kibi advice,
deep learning notes, Nebador citizens, and more, please see:

www.nebador.com

Nebador Archives
Kelso, Washington, USA

Although a Library of Congress Control Number was applied for, they failed
to issue one due to unknown circumstances within the Library of Congress.
If they belatedly succeed, it will be included in any future revisions and listed
on the NEBADOR internet site.

Manufactured in the USA

ISBN: 978-1-936253-90-6
NEBADOR10PBG: paperback, 6" x 9", 147 pages,
    global edition (10-point Georgia type)

Greetings, young people of planet Earth,

I must admit to being in a very strange mood, one that has lasted for many months, as I complete the final polishing of this book. To understand this mood, I must think back over the previous year of writing *Escape from Sonmatia Two*, coaxing the seven youth who attempted short stories for the Last NEBADOR Writing Contest, and finally helping the three who finished their stories to make them as good as possible.

Although we usually think of "moods" and other emotional states as stemming from human relationships, it appears that my current mood is coming from Mother Earth herself. During late 2015 and early 2016, some very unsettling news has begun to peek out of the usual noise of mostly-unimportant happenings around the world. These critical news items, completely ignored by the vast majority of people, are starting to make me think that my inspirations for the NEBADOR series are drying up at just the right time.

Mother Earth is changing, and she's not keeping it a secret. A thousand — maybe ten thousand — news stories could fit this description, but three rise above all the rest. First, she's getting hotter. As I write these words, the Earth has been experiencing record heat for twelve months in a row. Second, the floating Arctic ice cap is thinning and melting. It might look about the same, but it's in terrible condition and getting worse quickly. Third, just this spring the Carbon dioxide level in the air did a major jump upward that is hard to explain.

None of these three things has ever happened before, except maybe far back in deep geologic time. These three news items are telling me that slow, creeping climate change is NOT what is happening. Predictions for slight changes by the year 2100 are wrong. A new game is afoot, which is beginning to be called "climate disruption."

I hope all the NEBADOR stories will help prepare young people for the years ahead. I wish I could spend a week with each of you, showing you the joys of climbing a thousand feet in elevation, from the river to the ridge, to strengthen your bodies, or walking through the woods at night with coyotes yapping in the distance, to strengthen your minds. I will continue to teach and train the few young people, and their families, who are sent to me by the universe, and hope that these stories help the rest of you deal with the changes happening to Mother Earth.

J. Z. Colby
2016

Contents

"No mortal government, anywhere in the local universe, has ever faithfully represented its people. If one ever did, everyone in Nebador would just faint with surprise . . ."

— Feli-tala Rima

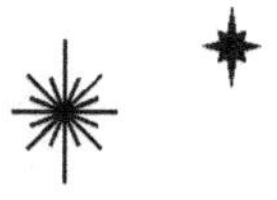

Part 1: Sonmatia One

The following short story is the First Place winner of the Last NEBADOR Writing Contest, 2014-2016.

Still Voices

by Mary Anne Brenner

This story takes place before, during, and after the visit of the Manessa Kwi to Sonmatia One in *NEBADOR Book Five: Back to the Stars.*

"Good Morning!"

"It's always morning here, silly crystal."

The young crystal giggled. "I know. Okay, Good Evening!"

"It's always evening, too," the older crystal said with a huff.

The young one frowned. "What if I said Good Afternoon?"

"Yikes! We'd be roasted back into stardust by the solar wind. No, thank you!"

"How about Good Night?"

"No! We'd be frozen solid and you couldn't even *think* enough to say Good Morning or anything else."

The young crystal sighed. "I guess I'll have to stick with Good Morning or Good Evening," she said.

"That would be nice," the older crystal said and went back to looking for stardust.

✳

"I caught one!" a double crystal, a little ways away, screamed.

"What's in it?" the young crystal asked, curious.

"Hmm. Let me see. Some silicon, a little calcium, and a bit of helium."

"Cool. Helium's sweet. Calcium's not bad. I caught a little a while back, when the stars were in slightly different places, and that big rock on the horizon was about twice as big as it is now."

"I caught a grain from it, back when I was smaller," another crystal said, searching her memory, "and it let me grow bigger."

"I hope I can catch enough grains of rock, or bits of stardust, to let me grow big someday," the young crystal said with longing.

❋

"Ooo!" the young crystal called out. "I just caught a grain from the horizon, with *two* bit of stardust stuck to it. Hmm, hmm. Lots of silicon, so I can grow a little bigger, and some calcium, hydrogen and helium, and . . . what's this? . . . could it be? . . ."

"What? Tell us!" many other crystal voices, mostly young, begged.

"It's . . . it's . . . carbon!"

"Way cool!" another crystal cheered.

"Those don't come along very often," an older crystal said.

"I'm going to save it for something special," the young crystal declared.

❋

In the middle of forever, that was always morning, and always evening, everyone had been silent for a long time. The young crystal could see her mother not far away, the big crystal that had caught enough stardust to grow another crystal on the side. It had fallen off when the ground shook, and the young crystal found herself alone, but still close enough to her mother to not feel lonely.

She could also see other small crystals nearby, her sisters, and a little farther away, a couple of big ones, her mother's sisters.

She looked up at the stars, and noticed that one of the shapes they made had changed since the last time she looked up.

"Caught one!" another crystal said. "Calcium and hydrogen."

Several crystals, including the young one, made sounds of happiness for their sister.

Once the celebration was over, the young crystal looked up again, and the stars had changed shape some more. She dreamed of catching more stardust someday, and while she dreamed, a hundred years passed in places where they had years.

❋

"Are the stars crystals too, like us?" the young crystal ask anyone who might know.

"I don't think so," her mother said. "They're much brighter than us."

"And different colors," a very old crystal said. "A few are a little bluish, like us, but mostly they're white or yellow. Some are even red."

"I guess you're right," the young one said, gazing up thoughtfully and noticing more changes in the shapes made by the stars.

❋

"What was that!" the young crystal gasped.

"What? Where?" several others wondered urgently.

"Something just swished by me, really fast!"

"Where is it?" her mother asked.

"I don't know . . . it's gone now. It was moving too fast to see. I didn't know *anything* could move that fast!"

"I saw a flash of light," the biggest, oldest crystal said, "but whatever made it was gone as fast as it came."

"Where are my sisters?" a very young crystal pleaded with worry in her voice. "I had two sisters near me, but now they're gone..."

"We're over here!" a pair of voices called from a long ways away.

The young crystal looked. "How did you guys get way over there?"

"At the same time as you saw something swish by, we felt something warm..." one said.

"And it was such a nice, perfect warmth that we were attracted to it, and stuck to it!" the other went on.

"But then it shook and we fell off. We went for a ride!"

"What do you think... half a meter?"

"Yeah, or maybe a little more!"

"Wow, I never *dreamed* I'd get to go on such a long journey!"

An older crystal frowned. "You're lucky your *journey* on that warm thing didn't take you into the light, where its too hot, or into the darkness, where its too cold."

"Yeah!" several other crystals agreed.

The two crystals were now about half a meter from where they would have spent the rest of their lives, if it wasn't for the fast-moving warm thing. They had no way to get back. The nearest other crystal was now almost a meter away. They looked at each other with worry.

But as the shapes made by the stars overhead changed again, the two crystals slowly settled down and realized how lucky they were. They had gone on an exciting journey. They were still in the part of the world where it wasn't too hot or too cold, and where grains of rock and stardust sometimes fell. And, best of all, they had each other for company.

✳

The two crystals who had gone on a journey became very close friends, since they were now so far away from everyone else. They had to talk really loud if they wanted the others to hear, and that tired them out, unless some stardust happened to fall to give them more energy.

"I remember something," one said after gazing up at the sky for a few centuries.

"What?" the other asked, also looking up.

"A feeling I sensed when the warm thing shook us off. I think it was... afraid of us."

"Afraid of *us?* That's pretty funny. We're just crystals, catching a little stardust, maybe a grain of rock now and then. How could anyone be afraid of *us?*"

"I don't know, but I think it was."

The two friends pondered this strange idea as they went back to watching the universe unfold.

✳

"I wonder if I'll ever get to go on an exciting journey," the young crystal wondered aloud somewhat after the middle of forever.

Her mother thought for a long time, and the stars changed places some more. "That is not our nature, little one. There are stars that glow brightly. There are the rocks that don't move and the solar wind eats them away slowly. There is the thing that swished by, made a flash of light, and carried two of your sisters half a meter. I have heard of other things that move, but have not seen them myself.

"We are crystals, able of witness the passing of the eons, and ponder the shape of the universe. As far as we know, we are the only ones who can do that. It is a good thing to be."

In the silence that followed, the young crystal felt comforted knowing that she and her sisters could do something that stars, rocks, and the fast-moving thing could not do. As the shapes made by the stars above changed again, she continued to catch stardust, and slowly forgot her dream of going on a journey.

✳

One day in the long stretches of forever, after the stars had changed their places a little more, something wonderful happened. A huge cluster of crystals, many times bigger than any that had ever grown from stray grains and stardust, was suddenly sitting in the sand. It hadn't crushed any of the other crystals, but was in a place crystals never grew because a big rock blocked all the incoming stardust.

"Wow . . ." many crystal voices said at once.

"Where did *you* come from?"

"How did you get so *big?*"

"Are you a crystal, or something else?"

"How did you grow so *fast?*"

The huge new crystal knew she had to think and speak very slowly. She was glad she had transferred all her work to other archangels before leaving Kerusemia.

"I am Dorolora. I'm not really a crystal, but I can take the shape of anyone I want to talk to. I'm an archangel, and I'm the head of Angel Services for the local universe of Nebador, which is your sun and all the nearby stars you can see in the sky."

"Wow . . ." the crystals, young and old, said again while looking up and saying the name they had never heard before. "Nebador . . ." The stars above changed places some more while the new name was whispered from crystal to crystal all the way around the planet.

"Some angels' helpers stopped here a while ago, and they noticed that you might be more intelligent and aware than just rocks . . ."

"Of course we are!"

"Rocks? How insulting to be compared to rocks!"

"We're *way* smarter than rocks!"

"Rocks are as dumb as they come!"

"We're *crystals*, the ones who watch the eons pass, collect stardust, and ponder the shape of the universe!"

Dorolora smiled to herself. "Yes, I can see that. Nothing like rocks."

During a moment of silence that was almost a year long, the young crystal found her courage. "I have a question."

"Yes, little one?"

"I think we remember your . . . angels' helpers . . . because they were the only things we've ever seen that moved so fast."

"Yes, they would have just been a blur to you."

"But we also remember that they were . . . this is embarrassing . . . they seemed to be afraid of us."

"Uh huh," the crystal who had felt the fear said. "How could anyone or anything be afraid of *us?*"

Dorolora chuckled. "It's just because they come from a world very different than this one, and would die here if they didn't have a ship and special suits. The same thing would happen to you if you went to their world."

"D-d-d-die, like a crystal that can't get any stardust?"

". . . and quits growing?"

". . . and goes dark?"

"Yes, like that. The angels' helpers who stopped here are called animals, and they need air and water and warmth, none of which you have here."

"Oh," the crystal said who had felt the fear.

"I guess that makes it okay," the young crystal said.

Dorolora looked at the young crystal for a long time. "How would you like to go on a journey, little one?"

"M-me?"

"You see, I am here for two reasons. First, I'm going to leave you an angel."

Another pretend-crystal appeared next to Dorolora, this one only slightly bigger than the oldest real crystals.

"This is Belasolia, and she's going to be your angel for a few million years, to watch over you and teach you about the universe."

"Belasolia . . ." the crystals began to whisper to each other.

Dorolora realized that they didn't know what a million years was. "Someday, a little later in forever, she will have to leave to learn new things and do other work, but then I will send you a new angel."

"So we'll always have an angel?" a large crystal asked. "And we can ask questions and the angel will teach us?"

"Always, I promise."

"Wow . . ." many crystals murmured.

"That'll be nice," the young crystal's mother said.

"But what about that journey you said something about?" the young crystal asked after she got over her shock.

"The other reason I'm here is to invite one of you, or maybe a pair of friends, to go see the local universe of Nebador. And someday, when you understand it well, you can help us with the work we do."

The young crystal didn't know what to say for a long time. The stars in the sky changed their shapes a little more, and Dorolora waited patiently, with Belasolia beside her.

"I . . . think . . . I know what . . . fear feels like . . . now," the young crystal finally said.

Dorolora smiled to herself, but remained silent.

"Will I . . . die?"

"Someday, as all mortals do, but not just because of your journey to see Nebador. We will give you a ship that will protect you any time you are in a place that's too hot or too cold."

"G-good. And . . . did you say I could bring a friend?"

"Yes. Almost all beings who help us with our work come in pairs, or trios, of sixes, or whatever is most comfortable for them."

"Can I bring my mother?"

"No. It would be best if your friend was about your age."

"Um . . . will someone . . . someone young . . . be my friend for a journey to see Nebador?"

Almost every crystal within hearing suddenly felt fear, and became slightly darker. The stars above moved some more, and Dorolora waited. After a long time, another young crystal, several meters away, slowly grew brighter. "I will!"

✳

It was a little ship, and it moved between the stars very slowly. That was on purpose, because its captain and steward needed lots of time to think about what they had seen.

Actually, the two crystals didn't understand the ideas of giving and taking commands, so they just took turns doing everything. The young crystal preferred the hydrogen-flavored stardust, and her friend preferred the helium-flavored, but they were both very happy, whichever stardust packet was open that century.

They never saw the same mammal, bird, reptile, amphibian, or insect twice. Every time they returned to a star station or planet station they had been to before, all of the mortal faces were new. But they were very happy to see Dorolora, Melorania, Belasolia, and other archangels and angels they came to know and love.

The pair of crystal friends became legendary, for somehow, in the centuries or millennia that they thought about the problems they were asked to study, they came up with solutions that no one else had thought of.

✳   ✳   ✳   ✳   ✳

Part 2

Escape from Sonmatia Two

This is a new novella by J. Z. Colby, based on the situation on Sonmatia Two that was described in *NEBADOR Book Five: Back to the Stars*.

Chapter 1: Dem's Dream

The boy thrashed in his sleeping niche, fighting with his blanket, then gained enough awareness to realizes he was just coming out of a dream. He sat up in the darkness and quickly felt re-connected with reality as the cool air chilled his slender, sweat-covered body, not quite fully-grown, but close.

A few feet away, on the other side of the small rocky cave, a hand removed the cover from a small glow-stone, revealing a concerned look on a girl's slightly-younger face. "You okay, Dem? Was it that dream again?"

Dem squirmed for a moment. "Yeah. You, me . . . a bunch of other kids, about a dozen in all, but I can't see exactly who . . . and miles and miles of tunnels and caves."

A moment passed before she made a rude noise with her tongue. "I'm your sister, remember. I've been sharing a sleeping cave with you since I was born. We have the same heartbeat. So I know when you're making stuff up."

Dem sighed and looked at the rocky floor. "Tir, I just can't tell you *everything*. You're not old enough!"

She rolled her eyes, then took on a stern expression. "I'm nine! And with that new law the Tunnel Thugs just made . . ."

"I know, I know. It's stupid, and it won't work, and everyone with half a brain knows that, but none of the Thugs . . . I mean our Honorable Government Leaders . . ."

Tir made the rude noise again.

". . . none of them *have* half a brain," he finished.

"You're being generous," she challenged. "I'd give them a quarter, max."

Dem took a deep breath. "No argument. I want to make one more try at finding the Pictures. I have a hunch where they might be hidden. I'm gonna look during my work shift tomorrow."

"If the quarter-brained Thugs didn't tear them up and burn them!"

"Actually, I heard they tried. But the Pictures wouldn't tear or burn!"

Tir laughed deeply.

Dem looked around warily. "Shhhh! If we're ever gonna have a chance of seeing my dream come true, we have to be very careful about who hears us."

She nodded, covered the glow-stone, and crawled back under her blanket. After hearing her brother get settled in his sleeping niche, she let another moment pass before asking, "The real part of your dream, or the part you made up?"

*　*　*

Chapter 2: Dem's Work

Dem put the next phase of his plan into action the following day. He felt a sense of urgency prompted by the announcement that the population had fallen below three hundred. The new law the Tunnel Leaders had enacted, so everyone would think something was being done about the problem, only made the urgency feel greater.

He arrived at work early and signed up for all the worst cleaning jobs — the ones that would allow him to look in the hiding places he had not yet checked.

Dem was not the only one who would like to see the Pictures again. Everyone remembered them, at least everyone out of diapers four years before when the Angels projected them onto the Gathering Cavern wall. He had been only seven at the time, but clearly remembered the anger on the Tunnel Leaders' faces. The Pictures themselves had quickly disappeared into the Government Tunnels where the leaders lived, made decisions, and kept all the best food for themselves.

Several of his friends had tried to find the Pictures, but had been caught and re-assigned to food-collecting teams. One was already dead from the toxic fumes outside, two more were sick and weren't expected to live much longer, and the rest just dragged themselves through each day, no longer caring about anything.

Dem had vowed to be more careful. He didn't really understand why the Tunnel Leaders were so against the offer the Angels made — a fresh, new planet where they could grow and hunt food, build houses in the open air, and live long enough to raise their children. But he was determined to *not* get assigned to food-collecting teams — at least until he turned twelve and had no choice.

So over the previous year, Dem had carefully worked his way onto the cleaning team — the handful of kids trusted to collect trash from all the

Government Tunnels, sort it, and give paper, food scraps, and anything else organic to the girls in the Mushroom Tunnels.

"Hey!" barked the voice of one of the minor leaders, a boy about fourteen or fifteen years old. "What are you doing?"

"Sorting trash, like I do every day," Dem replied, hoping the trembling he felt didn't show.

"How come I've never seen you in here before?"

"I usually work in the Planning Tunnel, but Jot is sick today, and Planning is still clean from yesterday, so I got his shift."

"Okay. I remember him coughing yesterday. We don't like people spreading germs in here. How old are you?"

"Eleven," Dem said, while continuing to sort the contents of a trash basket into the bins on his cart.

"As soon as the new law goes into effect next week, tens and elevens will start going outside for food collecting," the older boy said with a grin.

So you won't have to, Dem thought to himself. "I'm happy to do my part."

"You're the one with a sister, aren't you?"

Dem swallowed. "Yeah."

"She's cute, near the top of *my* list for mating as soon as the new law starts."

Dem remained silent and faced away from the other boy so the redness that covered his face couldn't be seen.

"Don't get any ideas about mating with her yourself before I get to her!"

"I'm not old enough for that."

"Good. Keep sorting that crap. Maybe if you do a really good job, you won't get put on a food-collecting team."

As the older boy wandered away, Dem continued to silently work. He had already decided that he was *never* going to help collect old canned food on the surface so the Tunnel Leaders could take the best of it and live easy lives until they died of old age at sixteen or seventeen. He would rather go live in the wild caverns and survive on slime mold and cave spiders.

But he still had a few places he wanted to look for the Pictures the Angels had left. And, of course, the Map.

✳ ✳ ✳

Chapter 3: Tir's Work

When Tir arrived at the Mushroom Tunnels that afternoon, she sighed. The morning shift had been very busy, and nearly fifty trays of soil awaited planting. Tir was a planter, receiving small spoons of spores from the sorters, older girls who worked with the microscopes to separate good mushroom spores from deadly ones.

Even though she wasn't old enough to be a sorter, Tir's job was highly-respected. An exhaled breath at the wrong moment could send a spoonful of spores onto the floor, hours of sorter time wasted, and the careless planter sent back to morning shift where the young and clumsy girls worked with anything organic — including things they didn't name but made jokes about — to prepare the mushroom soil.

Tir had become a planter as soon as she turned nine because she didn't talk much. The girls who couldn't keep their mouths shut also couldn't keep the spores on a spoon.

One of those mouthy girls worked on the same shift. Ril wasn't allowed anywhere near the spores, but was big and strong, so she hauled mushroom trays from the planting cave into the growing tunnels. She was there, already talking about everything and nothing, when Tir arrived.

"I am *so* excited about the new law! Our Leaders finally realized that eight and nine-year-olds are people, too, with needs and desires. I hope Dil will mate with me, like, anytime he wants! If I can't get him, Jak is my next choice, and I'm *sure* he'll want me after I wiggle my hips for him . . ."

Tir, getting her planting tools ready at her table, closed her eyes tightly for a moment and shuddered slightly. All of her tools were old kitchen utensils — spoons, forks, spatulas, and sifters. A spoonful of spores could easily plant five trays. Tir usually got six, sometimes seven. When she felt ready, she looked up and made eye contact with the planting supervisor at her desk.

Sim was twelve and very pregnant. Like Tir, she was quiet and careful, so had been a planter for years before becoming supervisor. She nodded respectfully when Tir looked at her. "Ril, Tir's ready for a tray."

Each tray, three feet long and two wide, weighed close to forty pounds. Without ceasing her chatter, Ril hoisted the first tray of the day, placed it on Tir's table, then went back for another as other planters signaled they were ready.

While waiting for spores, Tir looked at Sim. The supervisor's attention was elsewhere, so Tir could take a good, long look. Something was wrong with Sim's color. The faint light of the glow-stones didn't allow many skin tones to be seen, but even so, Tir frowned and her stomach tightened. She suddenly felt sure that neither mother, nor baby, would survive the upcoming birth.

Tir wanted to cry, but the arrival of her spores, on a spoon in a covered container, made her resist the temptation. She nodded thanks to the sorter, a serious girl of about thirteen, then glanced at the next planting table. Bel, the youngest planter at eight, was silently crying, but being very careful to not let it be seen.

Tir made a friendly hand motion in Bel's direction, than smiled slightly when she caught the younger girl's attention. She did her best to communicate with her eyes that they could talk at lunch, and Bel seemed comforted.

Tir turned her attention to the precious spoonful of mushroom spores and the tray of soil in front of her.

*

After Tir received a bowl of rejected mushrooms for lunch — edible but twisted and mixed up with bits of soil — she picked a quiet old tunnel, where she knew they wouldn't be overheard, and crawled into it slowly. Bel soon crawled in after, her own bowl in hand.

They picked the soil out of their lunch mushrooms in silence for a minute.

Eventually, Tir broke the ice. "What do you think of the new law?"

"Hate it!" Bel spat out, as if she had just accidentally eaten a big mouthful of mushroom soil.

Tir let the silence linger.

Eventually Bel found her voice again. "I like someone, but Fen's only nine . . . and now I'm going to have . . . all kinds of boys I *don't* like . . . trying to mate with me before . . . he even gets old enough . . ." Her voice trailed off into sobs.

Tir scooted close and put an arm around the eight-year-old.

Bel continued softly, her voice still mixed with deep sobs. "And I hate that someday . . . I'll probably have a baby from who-knows-which boy . . . and I probably won't live long enough to see it grow up . . ."

Eventually Bel's sobbing relaxed into silent tears, so Tir looked around, then spoke in a whisper. "Want to . . . get out of here before the new law takes effect?"

Bel's eyes snapped open wide and she looked at Tir while wiping her cheeks on a sleeve. "Really? Can I bring Fen?"

"Are you brave, and can you keep it secret for a few more days? Can *he* keep it secret, too?"

Bel nodded excitedly. "But . . . how?"

"Dem's pretty sure he can find the Angel Pictures . . . and the Map . . . today or tomorrow. We're leaving anyway. We'll find somewhere to live and be free . . . or we'll die . . . but we *won't* stay here where thugs force us to mate, and then keep all the good food for themselves, and . . . you know the rest . . ."

Bel nodded.

"I know three other girls who want to go, and Dem knows a couple of boys. Interested?"

Bel grinned.

*   *   *

Chapter 4: The Pictures

When Dem got off work and arrived home, Tir was crouching in the toilet corner, trying to wash the mushroom soil from her hands and arms with a rag and a bowl of water. When she looked up and saw the smile on her brother's face, she felt so excited that she knocked over the bowl. The water quickly disappeared into cracks in the rock.

"Oh, no! That was a quarter hour at the drip with four people in line yelling at me to hurry up!"

He knelt down near her. "It's okay. I found the Pictures — *including* the Map!"

Tir smiled while washing her hands with the moisture left in the rag. "I know four girls who will go with us, and one's bringing a boy. One says she'd rather jump off the balcony tunnel into the Gathering Cavern than start mating with boys."

"The new law starts next week . . ."

"I know, I know."

"And I found out today that boys ten and eleven will get assigned to food-collecting . . ."

"No, Dem! You'll die out there!"

"Maybe I'd be lucky and they'd let me keep sorting trash and garbage a little longer."

The girl didn't know what else to say, so she just dried her face on an old towel.

✴

Dem lurked out to the connecting tunnel to make sure no one was around before pulling the Pictures from his tattered old lunch bag. He spread them out on the stone floor as his sister's eyes grew wide with wonder.

"They were *really* well-hidden," he explained, "in a crack in the rocks behind the podium in the Council Chamber, covered by gravel. I covered it back up so no one will know they're gone."

"They'd *kill* you if they found out!"

"I don't plan to be here."

She nodded. "Dem, they're *beautiful!* I wish I'd been old enough to see them the first time. What *are* those giant things with lots of arms?"

"Those are called *trees*. Our world used to have them, up on the surface. I've seen drawings of them in the old books, before the Leaders quit letting us look at them."

"That color is so amazing. I don't think I've ever seen it before."

"It's called *green*. The Angels said that all the green creatures can make their own food from sunshine, and many of them have leaves, fruit, or seeds we can eat."

"Hooray! No more mushrooms!"

"I'm tired of them, too. It's been a year since I even *tasted* something from the old canned stuff that the food collectors bring in. The Tunnel Leaders keep almost everything for themselves now."

"You mean the Tunnel Thugs?"

"Shshshsh!" he warned, and slipped out to the connecting tunnel again to make sure they were still alone.

* * *

Chapter 5: Boys

When Dem got to work the next day, with three of the Pictures hidden in his lunch bag, he felt a deep sense of excitement and purpose. A large part of him wanted to tell *everyone* their plans, and get as many boys as possible signed up to storm out of there and leave the Tunnel Leaders to sort their own trash and find their own food on the surface.

Then he remembered the Map.

He and Tir had gazed at it for more than an hour, and they almost had it memorized. Some of the words on it started coming back to Dem as he prepared his trash-sorting cart for the day. It didn't say *Wide* Crawl-hole, it said *Tight* Crawl-hole. Not *Easy* Ledge, but *Dangerous* Ledge. No mention of *Straight*, *Level* Tunnels, but instead *Steep*, *Broken*, or *Choked* Tunnels.

Dem sighed as he pushed his cart toward his first cleaning job, and began thinking about the boys he most wanted to tell — thoughtful, quiet boys like himself — and how few of them, he now realized, could make the trip.

*

"Hey, Dil," Dem greeted as he joined others in the trash room at morning break. "You like challenges, don't you?"

"Damn straight!" the large, strong boy assured. "As soon as I'm thirteen, they'll let me be on the excavating crew. And I have *plans* for some of the eight and nine girls who are about to become mating age!"

Dem tried hard to hide his cringe while he looked around to see who else was in the room. One boy he didn't trust finished dumping his bins and left. The only other one was already signed up. "Dil, how would you like to go on a real, live adventure?"

"Real? Not one of those stupid little games the Tunnel Leaders put on that are *so* easy?"

"Totally real, with dangerous caverns, tight crawl-holes, sloping tunnels, all using a map no one has ever followed, and at the other end is a world where we can run on the surface, climb trees, hunt animals, and *everything!*"

"Count me in!"

"It's top secret until we leave in two days . . ."

"Nooooo problem!"

✳

When lunchtime had come and gone, Dem had invited two more boys he thought could make the journey. Bim, a strong ten-year-old, had accepted. The other had not, but Dem knew he would keep his mouth shut.

As he worked his way through the dreaded leaders' living area, Dem pondered who else to invite. His bins were soon full, so he headed back to the trash room.

Tik was an oddity. A tall twelve-year-old, almost thirteen, he was believed to have already gotten three girls pregnant, all of whom had asked *him* for the favor. But he never spoke — or at least, only enough to assure everyone that he could, and not a word more.

Dem decided to take the chance. At least there was little risk of Tik blabbing to anyone.

"Hey, Tik, I've got one of those sweet yellow mushrooms in my lunch bag. Want to split it with me? I've got something to talk to you about."

Tik nodded, and followed Dem into a small tunnel where they would not be overheard.

"Part of why I'm telling you this is you don't push yourself on girls who don't want you . . ." Dem explained as he broke the tasty mushroom down the middle.

Tik nodded as he received the gift and savored its sweet, nutty flavor.

While they both chewed, Dem brought out the Pictures he had hidden in his bag. He could see Tik searching them with his eyes, taking in the trees and animals, water flowing on the surface, and clear sky with scattered clouds.

"We're leaving in two days."

Tik nodded.

✳   ✳   ✳

Chapter 6: Preparations

Before collapsing into their sleeping niches that night, Dem and Tir divided up the remaining tasks. Dem could read far more words and symbols, so he would show the Map to their new traveling companions. Tir was in charge of supplies, which meant as many dried mushrooms as she could beg, borrow, or steal, and bags to carry them.

*

Tol, the quiet eleven-year-old cleaner that Dem considered a friend, gazed at the Map but only frowned. Dem pointed out various symbols and explained their meanings, but it didn't help. Finally, almost by accident, Dem discovered that when he described the tunnels and caverns in words, Tol began to glow with understanding.

"... then comes a long, winding tunnel with pretty cave formations and pools of water, before the next crawl-hole takes us to a small lave tube ..."

The only problem was, Dem had never actually seen any of the places he was describing, except the very first cave near the mushroom tunnels that contained a hidden crawl-hole. Even as he spoke, he worried that he was weaving a story that wouldn't turn out to be true. His words accurately depicted the shapes and lengths of the tunnels, and included all the information in the symbols, but still he worried.

Dem was about to admit his worry when Tol said, in a clear voice, "I can't remember all that, but I trust you to lead us!"

Dem took a deep breath, clasped hands with his friend, and said no more.

*

Tir met Dem for lunch, and she frowned deeply when he shared that Dil, one of his strongest and most reliable friends, wanted to ask mouthy Ril to come with them.

"That is *so* dangerous, Dem. She *cannot* keep her mouth shut, at any time, at any place, about anything."

Dem, not knowing much about Ril until that moment, breathed slowly for a moment, then nodded. "I'll make him promise to not even *tell* her about it until tomorrow morning, just before all of us don't show up for work."

"Can he handle that?"

"I think so. He *really* wants to go."

Tir nodded, and finished chewing her lunch mushrooms, but was still frowning as she returned to work.

✳

By late that afternoon, Tir discovered that Dil had *not* waited until the following morning, and Ril already knew about it. Tir was suddenly so clumsy at her work, she only got four planting trays out of a spoon of mushrooms spores. The supervisor looked at her sternly.

But eventually Tir noticed that somehow Ril managed to hide, just barely, what she was so excited about, except that it had something to do with Dil and mating. Everyone on the planet, all two hundred and ninety-five of them, already knew that much.

By quitting time that evening, Tir had to swallow her worry. Ril had managed to keep the details to herself, and the large, mouthy girl whispered to Tir that she knew the location of about twenty pounds of dried mushrooms.

Tir's eyes lit up. She had only been able to scrape up about ten pounds, plus one rusty can of something from the surface — "Spinach" the faded label said, whatever that was.

Tir smiled at Ril, for probably the first time ever.

✳

By that evening, Dem was very glad he had invited Tik.

The tall, silent boy peered at the Map intently, mostly agreed with Dem's analysis of the route through the tunnels and caverns, but also spotted some faint markings that made him frown. They talked about the possible meanings, Dem with words, and Tik with facial expressions, nods, shakes of his head, and an occasional word or two.

Somewhat to Dem's surprise, Tik didn't know any girls he wanted to include in the journey. The silent twelve-year-old became distant after that, with a half-smile on his face, as if remembering sweet times of the past. He soon waved good-night and wandered home.

✳

When Dem arrived at the sleeping cave he shared with his sister, he was surprised to find it completely quiet — so quiet he was almost startled that four girls were inside, working. Ril was even one of them.

"Shhh!" Tir warned as soon as her brother appeared in the entrance. "We're practicing. We know there will be dangers, and we plan to slip by them, as silent as cave mice. If we can get these dried mushrooms packed without the Thug Patrol hearing, then Ril will be in charge of food, Jin will carry the Angel Pictures, and Fim will bring extra glow-stones."

Dem looked around the little cave. Ril grinned happily from Tir's sleeping niche while tying a bag of mushrooms closed. Slender, wiry Jin, barely eight, looked at him with a straight face from the floor. Plump little Fim smiled from Dem's niche where she was filling another mushroom bag.

Dem smiled and sat down on the floor to help.

* * *

Chapter 7: Losses

The next day dawned like any other on Sonmatia Two. Only the Government Tunnels had any windows to the outside. The dozen departing middle-aged citizens of the only sapient civilization on the planet — varying from eight to twelve years of age at a time when the life-span had dropped to about seventeen — only knew it was morning because the Tunnel Patrols announced it in loud voices, like they did every morning.

The conspiring youth all squirmed with both excitement and fear while stretching and yawning in their little sleeping caves. Each was alone at the beginning of that day, except Dem and Tir, brother and sister, the only ones allowed to share a cave.

In most sleeping caves, glow-stones were uncovered, and scraps of mushroom saved from the previous night's dinner gave a little nutrition, knowing they wouldn't get any more to eat until they got to work.

But in a certain eleven sleeping caves, the excited residents knew they weren't *going* to work that day — or ever again. They were beginning a journey that might lead to better lives, or to Death itself, but at least not back to the boredom of their present miserable lives.

And they each had a shoulder bag containing several pounds of dried mushrooms — a huge treasure trove by their standards.

By previous agreement, knowing they would need their strength, they all started the day by chewing a large slice of dried mushroom from their bags, and washed it down with gritty water from one of the cave drips.

*

Of the dozen departing youth, Dil thought himself the strongest and most reliable. He knew Dem was better with the Map, Tik could think far ahead, and Fen could make everyone feel good with kind words, but Dil didn't think any of that was too important. He couldn't even bring himself to *imagine* what useful skills the girls had, other than mating. He knew Ril was looking forward to his passionate embrace, and was pretty sure Fim would also want him, in a year or two.

Even though everyone else had agreed on the need to carry their mushroom bags hidden under coats until clear of the patrolled tunnels, Dil thought that was pretty silly, slung his bag proudly onto his back, and strode out of his sleeping cave.

*

Min couldn't quit shaking as she got ready for work, then remembered she wasn't going to work.

Once she had finally gotten dressed in all her warmest clothes, and hidden her bag of dried mushrooms under them well, she found her feet taking her toward work, and had to stop herself and change direction without looking too suspicious. She mumbled something about forgetting a tool she needed, and the other girls in the passage waved and reminded her to not be late.

Her heart pounded in her chest as she slipped into a crack in the rock where she could be alone for a minute and think.

*

"Hey! What's in that bag?" the Tunnel Patrol yelled.

Dil froze. "Um . . . uh . . . lunch."

The Patrol started feeling and squeezing the bag that hung limply from Dil's shoulder. "Feels like two or three pounds. Anything over half a pound is considered hoarding."

Dil felt all the courage drain out of him, but forced himself to think. "Um . . . I don't work until this evening, so I was going on a long walk."

The Patrol spoke as he wrote on his note pad. "Two or three pounds, maybe four, to be determined upon inspection at the Patrol Station. Class B Hoarding, punishable by a month of food collecting . . ."

Dil's voice began to change from calm submission to hurt anger. "What's wrong with a big guy who gets hungry easy taking enough for a long walk?"

The Patrol glanced up but continued to write. "The suspect then became belligerent in the tunnels . . ."

*

Min, hiding in a nearby crevice, thought Dil was about to explode and pound the Patrol guy into mushroom soil. Part of her wished he would. But at that moment, two more Tunnel Patrols arrived and surrounded Dil. They took his mushroom bag, grabbed his arms, and led him off toward the Patrol Station as Dil's shoulders slumped and he hung his head in submission.

Min was shaking so badly she could hardly make her feet move, but somehow managed to slip out of the crack and stagger toward the old cave where all the departing youth were supposed to meet.

*

Dem, Tir, and the others listened. Fen and Bel held Min's hands and muttered comforting words. Ril sat alone, dealing with her own feelings of disappointment about Dil. Tik kept watch.

". . . and Dil *tried* to make them understand, but they just thought he was hoarding, and they're gonna make him go outside to collect food . . ."

Min eventually settled down, and most of the others thought she was going to be okay. Dem could tell she wasn't.

Just as Jin arrived in a big coat, with her bag of dried mushrooms hidden underneath, Min revealed her anguish.

"I'm . . . scared," she began in a shaking voice. "I . . . wanna go home."

*

For the next quarter hour, several people tried to coax Min to change her mind. Bel and Fen tried the hardest. They explained that they would be away from the Tunnel Patrols after just one crawl-hole, and the occasional Outer Patrols after only a day or so of travel.

Min remained petrified.

Finally someone mentioned that if she went back now, she'd only be a little late for work, and would probably go without lunch because of it, but nothing worse. If she stayed away much longer, then went back, she'd be in *big* trouble.

Min took one last shaking breath, handed her mushroom bag to those who would need it, and dashed toward the mushroom tunnels as fast as her stumbling feet could go.

* * *

Chapter 8: The Exit

The shock of the news about Dil, and then the departure of Min, lasted for several minutes.

A whiney voice finally broke the tense silence. "*Now* who's gonna be my mate?" Ril asked the universe with deep feeling and complete sincerity.

Bim, only ten, had never before imagined that he could succeed at something so grown-up, so manly, where someone like Dil, two years older, had failed. But he was strong, and growing fast. He looked around. None of the other boys, even Tik, appeared interested.

Bim smiled, first inwardly to himself, then for Ril. He saw her eyes sparkle a little, so he plucked up his courage, stepped beside her, and put his arm around her.

They looked at each other and both smiled.

Dem nodded. "I'm glad Ril has a mate. Now we have a crawl-hole to find."

✳

A sense of urgency came over the remaining ten travelers. The cave they were in was unused, since it contained only broken boulders, but they knew a Patrol could look in at any time.

Glow-stones, held by plump Fim, hovered over the Map. Dem, Tik, and serious little Jin searched it with their eyes. The crawl-hole should be near the back, on the right side, they agreed.

Once the Map was stowed, they crawled onto the rubble like scurrying cave rats. Bim started moving rocks that might be hiding their escape route. Tik received the stones and stacked them out of the way. Dem and his simple friend Tol poked around slightly farther back in the cave.

"Got it!" Bim announced, handing one more rock to Tik.

Ril beamed with pride as everyone gathered to look down into the hole.

"It's not a *crawl*-hole, it's a *climb*-hole!" Tir observed.

"With not an inch to spare," Bel added. "I'm not sure Dil could have made it."

Everyone looked at Bim and Ril, the largest boy and girl.

"I'm flexible!" Bim declared, trying hard to sound sure of himself.

Ril joined his mood. "I'll get though that hole if I have to *bleed* to do it!"

"Let's start with a scout to make sure it goes through," Dem said calmly. He looked at his sister, and she nodded.

✳

Tir, the first into the hole, was also the first to bleed from the task. Since she was only slightly larger than little Jin, no one, except maybe Jin herself, had any hope of getting through the hole unharmed.

She narrated her progress, and everyone listened, even Tik who kept an eye on the cave entrance. Everyone tried to remember the position of every boulder that would cut them to ribbons if they didn't bend or twist themselves just right at that point in the nearly-vertical downward climb.

About ten minutes later, which seemed like an hour to those listening, and three hours to Tir, she called up to her friends. "Whew! I'm in a large, old tunnel, fairly level. Lots of boulders from the broken ceiling. I *think* everyone can make it down if you take it slow and careful."

Bim and Ril clasped hands and silently looked at each other, gathering their courage, while Dem got all the small or slender ones started into the hole. Remembering Tir's narrative, most of them got through with only minor scrapes. Jin never seemed to even touch the rocks on the way down, except with her strong little hands. Mushroom bags and thick coats were tossed down separately.

Finally the large couple nodded that they were ready.

Dem asked Bim to go first, knowing he could best keep silent, even if wounded.

Ril, having now forgotten all about Dil, made sounds of pain and sympathy every time Bim cut or scraped himself.

Girls! Bim thought to himself, but continued to feel pride at having found a mate as he moved slowly down through the jagged hole, only breaking his silence to explain places where a twist of the hips or a sucked-in belly could avoid a cut or scrape.

✳

When Bim reached the old tunnel at the bottom, Ril almost danced around the exit cave with happiness, and Dem had trouble keeping her quiet. But when she finally settled down, she knew she had to do it. Her mate was at the bottom, waiting for her.

To Dem's eyes, Ril did try to remain silent, just as Bim had, but she was soon so cut and scraped that she was in real pain. Dem narrated every bit of warning advice he could remember, but Ril's painful sobbing didn't allow her to hear much of it.

More than half an hour passed as Ril filled the torturous hole, and when she could finally feel the tunnel floor at the bottom, she was covered with her own blood and crying deeply.

Dem glanced around the upper cave one last time, placed a rock where he could pull it over the hole once he was inside, climbed in, and disappeared from the world he had known.

*

When Dem got to the tunnel at the bottom, he became aware of several things at once.

Ril was sitting on a rock, crying loudly from the pain of her many scrapes and cuts, and sometimes nearly screaming, even though Bim was close beside her, trying to comfort her.

The light from a large glow-stone, the kind carried by Patrols, was moving in their direction about a hundred yards up the tunnel.

Everyone else looked very frustrated, nearly angry, with their feelings clearly directed at Ril.

Then something happened that surprised everyone. Tik spoke.

"There are probably several more crawl-holes like that."

Tir looked at Tik with wide eyes, but noticed serious little Jin give him a thumbs-up. A moment later, Tir nodded with understanding.

Because of the deep link they shared, suddenly Dem understood, too. This was the Moment of Truth for Ril and Bim — Ril had to either master herself, or return to the world she knew.

"No, I can't go through that again!" Ril shrieked, then began crying once more.

Bim, still beside Ril and holding her tightly, looked up at the others. "I'll stay with her, deal with the Outer Patrol and everything."

Quiet Bel cocked her head. "They've bonded, like me and Fen."

A few seconds of silence passed.

"Everyone else," Dem said firmly, "hiding places, glow-stones covered."

Bim tossed his mushroom bag to Tol as the remaining eight travelers scurried to find places to hide from the approaching Patrol. Then he returned to comforting his new friend and mate.

* * *

Chapter 9: Outer Patrols

The Outer Patrol was sympathetic when they saw Ril's many cuts and scrapes. Bim did, of course, mutter a half-way reasonable story about looking for a place to be alone with Ril and accidentally following the *wrong* crawl-hole. The Patrol led the couple back to the populated tunnels with only a severe warning and the usual consequences of being late for work. They also warned the pair to not get caught mating until the new law took effect three days later.

The other eight friends crept out of their hiding places and uncovered glow-stones.

"I think Tik did the right thing by scaring Ril," Tir shared. "It would have been much worse if this happened a day or two into our journey."

Most everyone else nodded.

Tol didn't quite understand what had happened, but held up the extra bag. "More mushrooms!"

Dem smiled at his simple friend.

✳

The tunnel was a natural lava tube about thirty feet high. It had once had a fairly smooth floor, but now was strewn with boulders, and sometimes piles of boulders, from thick layers of rock that had fallen from the ceiling.

A well-worn path snaked among the boulders, showing that the tunnel was regularly patrolled.

The travelers studied the Map as they chewed dried mushrooms. Dem and Tir guessed they had several hours of tedious walking before they would be free of the danger of Outer Patrols.

Tik and Jin made eye contact and both nodded.

Tol yawned.

✳

The group didn't get far before a Patrol forced them to scramble behind boulders again. Everyone did a good job of staying as quiet as cave mice while the clueless Patrol passed.

It happened again less than a quarter hour later.

The third time caused words and noises of frustration as soon as the Patrol had moved on.

"*Why* so many *Patrols?*" Tol wondered aloud.

"A bunch of people didn't show up for work today," Tir explained patiently, "over and above the four who were just a little late."

Tol looked puzzled as they made ready to take to the path again. About a minute later, he suddenly stopped. "Oh, you mean us!"

Tik smiled at him.

✳

With all the time spent hiding and waiting for Patrols to pass, the group's progress was painfully slow. As the sixth Outer Patrol was passing, plump little Fim was becoming impatient where she hid behind a large boulder with Jin. She shifted her leg too quickly, felt a twinge of pain from a sharp rock, and gasped.

"Who's there?" the Patrol called, uncovering a bright glow-stone.

Jin sighed to herself, dropped her mushroom bag, then stood up and pretended to limp toward the Patrol.

"What're you doing down here?"

"Running away from a big *goon* who wanted to mate with me before it's legal. Then I stepped on a sharp rock."

"Have you seen anyone else? A bunch of cleaners and mushroom growers are missing."

"Nope, not down here."

"You're on report, and will probably have to work a double shift."

"Anything to keep me away from that *goon*."

"Let's go."

✳

Fim began shedding tears of guilt when it was finally safe to do so. Everyone crept out of their hiding places and uncovered glow-stones.

Bel and Fen, holding hands for mutual comfort, both looked sad. "We lost another one," Bel moaned.

Tik shook his head.

Seeing that, Dem and Tir looked at each other and both smiled with understanding.

"I think we need a break to eat and look at the Map," Dem began. "What do you think — a quarter hour?" he asked, looking at Tik.

Tik nodded.

✳

Jin pranced up the path from the climb-hole about ten minutes later.

"How did you do it?" both Fim and Tol asked her.

"The only power the Thugs have is a little shame and taking away a meal or two," Jin began. "What are they going to do, stop me from going to work cutting mushrooms? People would starve! What do I care if I'm on report, people look at me funny, or I'm supposed to work a double shift? I don't *live* there anymore. I put your rock back over the hole before climbing down," she finished, looking at Dem.

"I'm *so* sorry!" Fim blubbered. "I promise I won't do it again!"

"That save was free," Jin said. "Next time, you're on your own."

Fim nodded acceptance of the warning.

Tik smiled at Jin.

✳ ✳ ✳

Chapter 10: Zero-Tolerance Situation

After successfully hiding from two more Outer Patrols, the group of rebels finally reached the point where the Map said they should leave the big lava tube. It described a tight crawl-hole on the right side, and a wide but low belly-crawl that made everyone moan, feeling scraped hands and knees in advance.

The crawl-hole was horizontal this time, but they almost wished it was another climb-hole, as it had no level floor. Scraped skin oozed blood, and they hadn't yet arrived at the belly-crawl.

While chewing dried mushrooms, they remembered hearing stories that once, long ago, ointments had existed that could sooth and heal scraped skin. None of them had ever seen such a thing, and agreed that if they ever existed, they had run out long ago, or were kept under lock and key in the Government Tunnels.

Tir and Jin made rude noises.

*

The belly-crawl, as they suspected, was on solidified lava. It looked smooth from a distance, but was just rough enough to open all the scrapes and cuts on their hands and knees, and add many new ones.

Their faces were not exempt, and anyone who dared to rest their heads for a moment, paid the price. The section of one-foot-high tunnel was only about twenty feet long, but took two hours, and all their energy.

*

Dem licked his hands. He knew it was necessary to keep them from getting infected, but couldn't stop himself from cringing from the stinging sensation while they dried. Finally, he got out the Map.

After finishing her own licking, Fim brought their brightest glow-stone close.

"Unless there's another way to this point, we're done with Outer Patrols."

"Hooray!" several people cheered.

Tik just nodded.

"Now we have a Dangerous Ledge," Dem explained.

"Ah! Ledges are easy!" Tol asserted.

Tir waited a moment before speaking. "We'll see."

Dem looked around. Everyone was dead-tired, but their current location was nothing but sharp rocks. "We need to rest and sleep soon . . ."

"Not here!" Bel moaned. "No one would get any sleep on *this*. We need some nice, soft sand."

Fen, Tol, and Fim agreed quickly with nods. Tir, Tik, and Jin looked less sure, but didn't say anything.

Dem was very uncomfortable with the idea of traveling again after the hours of hiding they had endured, and the many cuts and scrapes they had all received, but didn't feel he had the right to ask them to sleep on sharp rocks.

✳

The so-called ledge turned out to be a series of barely-visible handholds and footholds on the wall about twenty feet above a pit with twisted rocks at the bottom.

Even Tol saw the risk. "Yep. *Dangerous* Ledge. But we can do it."

Tik wore an intense frown.

"No way around?" Tir inquired when the Map was out again.

Dem studied it, with Fen and Jin looking on. "Not that we know of."

Tir took a deep breath while placing her glow-stone in a shallow pocket so she would have both hands free.

During the next few minutes, everyone else finished chewing mushrooms and did the same.

✳

Feeling a burden of responsibility for the others, Dem went first, and narrated the size and location of every handhold and foothold, especially when gaps forced him to stretch.

Tol came next, feeling confident that he could handle the so-called Dangerous Ledge.

Tir followed, adding a girl's perspective to the narration.

Plump little Fim looked at Tol, who was having no trouble with the crossing, smiled, and took the first handhold.

Bel started across next, then Fen.

Without warning, and at first without any sound, Fim disappeared. For a moment, she was merely surprised that her hand had slipped off the next handhold. Another fraction of a second later, it dawned on her that her trailing hand hadn't held either. By then, she was half-way to the bottom.

The others heard a forlorn cry just a split-second before a heavy thud. Everyone else froze where they were, and complete silence filled the cave.

With his heart in his throat, Dem got a secure grip with one hand and pulled his glow-stone from his pocket. Farther back in the line, Fen did the same.

Fim was face down, her neck and one leg twisted at weird angles, blood quickly covering the rocks under her.

Tol looked, immediately started crying like a baby, and didn't pay any more attention to his handholds.

Tir, just behind him, saw Tol's state of mind, quickly got a good grip and threw her free arm around him.

Dem dropped his glow-stone and did the same from in front of Tol. "Everyone, please watch your hand and footholds . . . stay where you are until you feel ready to move . . . don't even look down if you can help it."

✳   ✳   ✳

Chapter 11: Ups and Downs

Tol remained in shock and grief. It took Dem and Tir nearly half an hour to coax him the rest of the way across the Dangerous Ledge. All that time, Bel and Fen clung to the wall, tempted to go back, but staying where they were in hopes that the way would soon be clear. Finally, they were able to get across.

Jin, then Tik, crossed very carefully while Tol sat between Dem and Tir, crying his eyes out.

"I . . . didn't even know . . . I liked her . . ." Tol was eventually able to share between sobs.

Some of the others were tempted to smile, but didn't.

*

Once they had settled down, everyone but Tol crawled back to the edge and looked into the pit. Dem's dropped glow-stone, and Fim's three, illuminated some of the blood, now turning brown. She lay completely still, exactly as she had landed.

They talked, and agreed that climbing into the pit would be extremely dangerous. They weighed that danger against the lost mushroom bag and glow-stones. No one was in the mood to risk another accident. With wrinkled brows, they agreed that they had enough mushrooms and glow-stones to go on.

They experienced Fim's death on two levels. They grieved for their friend and companion. They were also aware that every death, in a civilization of less than three hundred people, brought them a big step closer to extinction.

Now they had to sleep, and the floor of the lava tube was no better than before the pit. Bel and Fen curled up close to each other, but got little sleep. Tol just tossed and turned while mumbling things he remembered about Fim. The others might have dozed off for an hour or two, but without any Patrols to announce work shifts, it was hard to be sure.

*

When Dem eventually sat up and rubbed his eyes, he looked around. Jin and Tik appeared to be the only ones who had figured out how to get comfortable on the rocky floor. A moment later, Tik sat up and stretched, then came over and joined Dem. They both opened mushroom bags to see what was for breakfast.

Suddenly, Dem realized the problem. "Where's Tol?"

Soon, everyone was up, trying to remember when they had last seen him, or heard him sniffling. Hours before, they all agreed.

Dem and Tik both had the same initial, frightening thought, and dashed back to the edge of the pit.

Fim was still there, silent as the rocks. No sign of Tol was to be seen.

Tir and Jin found him just a hundred or so yards farther along the tunnel, sitting on the hard ground, hugging his knees, rocking back and forth while muttering to himself. He came willingly, but without joy or purpose, when they coaxed him to return to the group and eat some mushrooms with them.

*

The path the Map wanted them to follow that day was long and winding, but with no labeled dangers. A few symbols baffled them, and some arrows pointed in different directions, sometimes the way they were going, sometimes back.

"What does *that* mean?" Fen wondered aloud.

Tik looked thoughtful. No one else had a clue.

At Dem's suggestion, they took stock of their resources. Only six glow-stones could be found, one less than people. Bel offered to go without and stay close to Fen.

The mushroom supply looked like it would last several more days.

"We really need to find water," Tir asserted, having difficulty swallowing the mushroom she was chewing.

Everyone nodded, but had no idea when that would happen.

*

Tol had to be prodded nearly every step of the way. All hope seemed to have left him, and he just sat down and hugged his knees every time they stopped to rest, look at the Map, or when they simply forgot to prod him. Most everyone was soon trying to avoid the task. Dem took over to keep his friend moving.

Although no dangers presented themselves, the lava tube was soon going steeply downhill, causing unsure footing among the sharp rocks that littered the floor.

Although the lava tubes tended to be fairly straight, not so the limestone cave they discovered after a short, easy crawl.

They stood up as they entered the cavern, one by one, and gazed around in wonder at the stone draperies, slender stalactites, and bulging stalagmites all around them.

Tol sat down and looked at the ground.

They knew about limestone caverns because parts of the inhabited tunnels were once decorated by the same beautiful stone formations. Centuries of hands, feet, and excavation had destroyed most of the beauty, but enough remained that the travelers knew the names of the strange stone shapes.

The sound of dripping water soon called them to a pool where they all drank deeply. Dem had to almost force Tol to drink, but kept his frustration to himself.

*

The way before them, although made beautiful with stalactites and other formations, was now winding and hard to follow, so they looked at the Map often. Tir realized that the arrows always pointed up-slope, so they could see in advance that they would be going up and down all day long.

Mostly down.

The twisting limestone cavern had been carved by an underground river countless centuries before, then decorated by dripping mineral water after the river dried up. That river had not been too concerned with going in a straight line, nor afraid to plunge into deep places before bubbling up again somewhere else.

The travelers could follow the twisting and turning on the Map without too much trouble.

The ups and downs were harder to navigate, and often sand half-filled the low places.

So they chewed mushrooms, drank from crystal-clear pools nestled among towering stalagmites, and prodded Tol to keep going, hour after hour, occasionally up a little, but mostly deeper and deeper into the planet.

*

Tir thought she was just tired as they stumbled down a slope between stone draperies. Then she realized the air was starting to smell bad, and noticed that everyone else was having trouble breathing, too. Tik and Jin made eye contact with her and nodded. Dem quickly joined in the realization of what was happening, and explained it to the others who hadn't guessed.

"That's like ... in the lowest storage caves ... under the Government Tunnels ..." Fen shared, "... where they keep the canned food. No one works ... in there for more than ... a quarter hour at a time."

Jin nodded. "Bad air sinks."

Dem got out the Map and they all gathered close — except Tol, who just hugged his knees and rocked.

"Oh, no!" Tir moaned. "More *down* before ... it starts to go *up*."

"Do we have ... any choice?" Dem asked anyone who cared to answer.

Most just looked at each other. Tik shook his head. Tol rocked.

*

The longest hour of their lives began, and felt like six hours. In the deepest part of the cave system, where the underground river had carved a smooth but winding tunnel through the rock, bad air collected. Some was probably Carbon dioxide, the natural result of all breathing, burning, and decomposition. The sickly smell might have been pollution that lingered from the industrial civilization that once covered the surface of Sonmatia Two.

Gasping, they pushed forward, knowing that any other path to their destination might take weeks to find. Some were tempted to run, but the lowest places, choked with sand and gravel, forced them to hunch over, crawl, and even dig in one place.

Panic was close, and getting closer.

To add to their problems, Tol wanted to sit down and withdraw from the world more and more often. Dem forced him to keep going with pokes, prods, and eventually threats of violence. Tol responded weakly to the prods, but didn't seem to hear the threats.

Every slight uphill brought hope, but those always seemed to be followed by an even-longer downhill.

The group didn't dare stop. They knew their survival in this place was measured by time — minutes, not hours.

Tir tried to keep an eye on everyone. Fen and Bel stayed attached to each other, but both were turning blue and stumbling often. Tik couldn't seem to get enough air, no matter how deeply he breathed. Dem and Jin were not much better. Only Tol seemed unconcerned, but that, Tir knew, was because he no longer cared whether he lived or died.

They didn't dare stop to consult the Map, so they were hardly aware of going up again. With his last burst of determination, Dem pushed Tol to keep walking. Jin pulled Tik along. Bel and Fen dragged each other. Tir somehow managed to keep putting one foot in front of the other.

Suddenly Tik stopped and shared a few of his rare words. "I can breathe!"

✳ ✳ ✳

Chapter 12: One More

Rejoicing in every breath of the sweet air, they staggered forward, happy with every step, no matter how difficult, that took them higher and higher in the twisting and turning limestone cave system.

As soon as they felt dry sand under their feet, they fell down, mumbled something that might have been *Good Night*, and slept.

*

Many hours later, Dem woke from his deep, dreamless slumber. Tir was near, still sleeping. Fen and Bel were snuggled close together. Tik and Jin were not far apart. Tol was . . .

"Damn! Where's Tol *this* time?"

Hearing him, Tir and Jin stirred. Tik soon sat up. They all stood, stretched, and looked around.

The sand that had given them a comfortable place to sleep had piled up at the entrance to a large cavern. Several fat stalagmites loomed on the edge of their dim glow-stone light.

Dem noticed Fen stirring. "Fen and Bel will guard the mushroom bags. The rest of us, let's search this cavern for our troubled friend."

As the four searchers held their glow-stones high and each went a slightly different way among the cave formations, they were all hoping the same thing — that they would soon find Tol, and that he hadn't gone back the other way.

*

Since the cavern was only about a hundred feet across, the searchers soon found each other and the exit tunnel, its floor covered with wet sand. Tik crept about slowly, his glow-stone held low to examine the sand. Finally he walked back to the other three, shaking his head.

"Damn!" Dem said again. "That means he . . ."

"Yeah," Tir agreed.

They returned to Fen and Bel, who had breakfast ready. Everyone started chewing dried mushrooms.

"I'm not surprised," Tir admitted after swallowing. "He lost the will to live."

Jin nodded. "I think it started *before* Fim died."

Dem thought while he chewed and swallowed. "Tol is a wonderful, happy guy when life is simple."

"I think it quit being simple enough," Bel shared, "when they made that new law. At least . . . that's what ruined it for *me*."

"Yeah," Fen agreed. "That was a sign that . . . our pitiful little world was in big trouble."

Tik and Jin nodded.

The six travelers fell silent and continued chewing mushrooms.

✳

Since Tol had been Dem's friend, he didn't feel good about continuing the journey without one more attempt to find the lad. Tir and Jin tried to talk Dem out of doing what he was about to do, but couldn't. Tik nodded with understanding.

Dem breathed deeply for a minute to get as much good air into his body as possible, then headed back along the winding tunnel at a fast walk. He knew about where breathing would become difficult, and didn't plan to go much farther. Tol hadn't been *that* good a friend.

Gasping and feeling light-headed, Dem found Tol curled up on the sand not far into the bad air. He would have liked to sit with his silent friend for a hour. Instead, he took the glow-stone from Tol's stiff hand, whispered *Good-Bye*, and trudged back toward the life-giving air.

✳   ✳   ✳

Chapter 13: A New Way to Travel

The six remaining companions now had a glow-stone for each person, and plenty of dried mushrooms for several more days. After those were gone, they had no idea what they would eat, so didn't even bother discussing the topic.

After Dem had fully regained his breath, he sat down and got out the Map. Everyone gathered around.

"I think we're about half-way there," Tir observed.

Dem scrunched his face for a moment, then nodded weakly.

"What're those wiggly lines?" Bel asked.

"Don't know," Dem admitted. "Wiggly rocks?"

Tir and Fen shrugged.

Tik opened his eyes wider, but didn't say anything. Only Jin noticed.

✳

After mushrooms were chewed and everything packed, a leisurely walk brought them to the wet sand at the other end of the cavern they had already explored.

Dem took one more look back toward the final resting place of his simple friend, then led the group into the new tunnel.

The wet sand descended gently, but the air remained good, almost fresh. The sand, however, got wetter and wetter. Soon it made a squishing sound as they walked.

The tunnel they followed — the only tunnel that matched the route shown on the Map — curved this way and that, and continued to go down slightly or stay level. As easy as the going was, all six travelers were soon frowning.

The shoes on their feet were hundreds of years old, and had been handed down from generation to generation. Most were wrapped and patched with materials salvaged from the surface — lengths of string and wire, or pieces of leather and plastic. Used carefully, those shoes protected their feet from the cold, hard rocks of the inhabited tunnels.

Now the travelers were sloshing through liquid water an inch deep, rapidly approaching two inches. Their old shoes had no hope of keeping that water out, and several pairs were threatening to fall apart.

"Damn!" Tir moaned as her shoe stayed in place and her bare foot came out when she tried to take a step.

Dem picked it up and handed it to her.

She took off her other shoe and wiggled her bare feet in the water. "As long as it's just sand, who needs shoes?"

The others smiled and followed her lead.

✳

From cracks in the walls, more water joined that oozing up through the sand, and the travelers soon found themselves wading through half a foot of water flowing in the direction they were walking.

At the same time, the ceiling of the tunnel became lower and lower.

During the next quarter hour, with deep frowns on all six faces, and hearts pounding in their chests, the water became two feet deep, and the ceiling began scraping their heads in places.

Dem stopped and looked around at his companions. If there had been any point in stopping, looking at the Map, and talking about their route, he would have been the first to propose it. But he could see no point in doing any of that, so he trudged onward through the swirling water.

Finally, they came to the end.

The underground river was now three feet deep, and within the light of their glow-stones, the ceiling came down and met the water.

✳

For several long minutes, they all stood silently in the cold, flowing water, some of them starting to shiver.

Dem went as far forward as he could with his glow-stone held high. There was no gap — the water filled the tunnel completely. He returned to the others.

Tir sighed deeply. "It's a *long* way back, with no way around . . . that we know of. There might *be* one, but we could spend *weeks* looking for it."

Bel had tears on her cheeks. "We've got mushrooms for maybe . . . three or four days. I haven't even seen a cave spider!"

They all stood in silence for another minute.

"I'm going on," Jin suddenly said firmly.

Everyone looked at her.

"I knew I might die on this journey. I think looking for another way to the Angels' camp is a fool's hope. If the Map says this is the way, then this is the way I'm going."

After a long silence, Tik nodded. No one else was quite sure if he was just nodding out of respect, or was agreeing with Jin.

"I . . . agree with everything Jin said," Dem forced out with his heart in his throat. "The water must be those wiggly lines on the Map, and we're only supposed to leave this tunnel after going along with the wiggly lines — the water — for a ways."

With big, round eyes, Fen looked at Dem "How long is *a ways?*"

Dem was slow to answer. "I . . . don't . . . know."

*

Dem could see that Tir was okay. She was breathing deeply, and he knew that was her way of gathering her courage for something hard. He also knew Tik was becoming fond of serious little Jin, and would most likely join her in voting to go forward. Bel and Fen, however, worried him.

In the silence that lingered, Bel started openly crying and talking at the same time. "But the mushrooms'll get wet and rot!"

Dem let some silence linger while Bel's tears ran their course. "You're right. If our mushrooms get wet, we'll have no more food very soon."

"I'm still going," Jin asserted. "Before they rot, we can eat all the mushrooms we can cram into our bellies."

The others saw the wisdom in Jin's statement, but felt no joy, since they didn't really *like* mushrooms. It was simply the only food available most of the time.

Fen took a deep breath and put his arm around Bel. "It's through the water with our friends, or a long journey back through the bad air to our old lives . . ."

"Where you'd be in *lots* of trouble!" Jin pointed out.

Fen nodded toward Jin, then looked into Bel's eyes again. "Whatever you decide, I'm with you.

Bel burst out crying again.

*

With everyone, including Bel, starting to shiver, her tears eventually faded and she looked at Fen. "You think we should go through the water, don't you?"

He blinked several times before he could answer. "Yeah. I don't think the Angels would have given us a bad map, and I think I'd rather die with my friends than die in a few more years from the poison air outside while collecting old food for the Government Thugs.

Bel smiled at his use of the term Tir usually used. "Then . . . then I'll die with you . . . or maybe . . . who knows? . . . find the Angels . . ."

Dem went into action. He knew they wouldn't be able to swim, or stand up, or anything else if they got any colder. "Okay, mushrooms bags across to your opposite shoulders so they won't fall off. Glow-stones in one hand tightly. The other hand feels the ceiling, and as soon as there's enough air, stop, breathe, and see where you are. Because of the current, no one will be able to come back and tell anything, so everyone has to make their own decision and live with it." He thought about adding *or die with it*, but decided not to.

After his mushroom bag was secure, and he saw that the others had all done the same, he went on. "You are all the best friends . . . and best sister

. . . anyone could have."

Tir smiled.

Tik and Jin, standing side by side, nodded their respect of their trusted leader.

Fen and Bel just held each other tightly.

Dem took a final deep breath, flopped into the water, and let the current take him into the cold, dark unknown.

✳ ✳ ✳

Chapter 14: More Losses

Dem quickly realized he had been completely wrong.

Within a few yards of entering the tunnel, the underground river became much narrower, deeper, and faster.

Dem couldn't touch the bottom with his feet. His free hand struggled to feel the ceiling, but only succeeded for a moment every few seconds. Grabbing anything, to stop himself from moving helplessly along with the water, became impossible.

Suddenly, plenty of air appeared above him, and the river slowed a little. Surfacing and spitting water, he took a deep breath and beheld a sandy shore on the left side of the river.

Since Dem had grown up without ever seeing a river, lake, or ocean, only an instinctive dog-paddle allowed him to move toward the shore. Meanwhile, the river was determined to pull him into the next tunnel, again filled to the ceiling with water.

Swim out now! a little voice seemed to whisper loudly and urgently in Dem's mind.

He paddled with all his might, and felt sand under his feet at the far end of the little beach, just before the river plunged into darkness again. But each step he tried to take gained little, until desperation made him drop onto his hands and knees.

Finally, he crawled, inch by inch, up the sand with the water still trying to undermine each step and pull him into the next flooded tunnel.

✳

Dem lay on the sand, breathed, and lost track of time.

Less than a minute after he arrived, Tir broke the surface and sputtered.

Without thinking, Dem jumped to his feet and dashed to the downstream end of the beach. "Swim out! I'll try to grab you, but you've got to get out of the current!"

He saw Tir frantically dog-paddling, felt the sand under his feet become unstable, and reached out as far as he could. "Yes! Just a little more! Reach!"

Tir's free hand met his, she struggled to get firm sand under her knees, and was finally able to crawl out of the water.

Brother and sister hardly had time to exchange any more words before Fen and Bel appeared, holding onto each other with one hand, clutching glow-stones with the other. As soon as they surfaced, they seemed to recognize the shore and their two companions, but fear showed on their faces and they couldn't make any progress swimming.

"Let go of each other and SWIM!" Tir screamed.

Dem moved to the far end of the beach again to try and grab them.

The pair in the water were slow to release their holds on each other, and a second passed before they did. During that second, they remained powerless to move toward the beach, and the river had its way.

Dem reached out as far as he could, but the couple was swept into the far tunnel without any chance of stopping.

Tir was tempted to cry, but events were moving too quickly. Jin appeared in the water.

Dem stayed at the far end of the beach. "Swim out NOW!" he yelled.

"Come on, Jin, you can do it!" Tir screamed, determined to not lose another one.

Jin was strong for her small size, and quickly sized up the situation and began paddling fiercely. She made the beach without needing help from Dem.

Tik broke the surface and shook the water from his face.

"SWIM OUT!" the three on the beach yelled.

Tik seemed clumsy in the water, and began coughing while he tried to swim.

Dem knew it would be close, so he took one more step into the water.

Tik's dog-paddle was weak at first, then he managed to get his legs onto the surface and kicked wildly.

"Reach!" Dem yelled just as Tik approached the end of the open water and was in danger of being swept downstream.

Their hands met, Dem held his ground, Tik struggled to get his knees under him, and he finally felt enough firm sand to begin crawling up the beach.

They all flopped onto the sand and just breathed for a long minute.

Eventually, Jin found her voice. "Where's Fen and Bel?"

Chapter 15: Moving On

No one knew where Fen and Bel might be, or even if they were alive or dead.

Dem quickly got out the Map. It showed very little outside the one path they needed to follow, and nothing of the course of the underground river beyond their current location.

"There's probably another beach not far along, and next time, they'll be ready to swim," Dem said with all the hope in his heart.

"Any maybe their new path will cross our path, and we'll be together again!" Tir added.

Tik and Jin nodded, but remained silent.

"Okay, countdown," Dem announced. "Dried mushrooms that get wet start molding in half a day, and are poisonous in about one day."

"Or less," Jin pointed out with a dark expression on her face.

Tik nodded, and everyone opened their soggy mushroom bags and started eating like it was their last meal.

*

They knew, from the Map, that their little beach sat on the edge of a large cavern. When they finally climbed to the top of the sandy slope and held glow-stones high, they were amazed to discover massive stalagmites, ten or fifteen feet across, that soared high above them, often connecting to thick stalactites above. All four travelers nearly fell over with dizziness as they struggled to glimpse the cavern ceiling, somewhere beyond the reach of their lights.

"Wow . . ." Tir breathed.

"I didn't know they *got* this big!" Dem declared.

Jin felt overwhelmed and frowned.

Tik just smiled.

The walls of the huge cavern also quickly receded from view, both to their right and left, and the far wall was nowhere to be seen among the giant cave formations.

After looking in every possible direction, Dem focused on the right-hand wall of the cavern. "That wall's closest to the river. Maybe we'll find another beach, and there will be Fen and Bel, eating mushrooms."

The others nodded, then forced themselves to take another bite of soggy fungus.

✳

The journey through the great cavern, as close to the right-hand wall as they could go, turned out to be difficult and slow. Sometimes thick stalagmites almost formed impenetrable fences. In other places, stone draperies forced the travelers to go around, or belly-crawl underneath. In between those obstacles, slippery flowstones — where the cave formations had just spread out on the floor or a gentle slope — made walking and climbing dangerous.

After several hours of painfully-slow progress, they came to a small sandy area, but had seen no sign of the underground river, nor any tunnel that might lead to it.

Tir flopped onto the sand. "I am *so* tired! I am going to sleep a little. You can go on without me, or you can carry me. Good ni . . ."

Dem smiled. In a pinch, he could carry little Jin, but not his sister. Before giving in to sleep, he climbed to the top of the next rise and looked ahead. Tik silently joined him. Neither could see or hear any hint of the river that had carried away their friends.

They returned to the sandy place and joined the girls in dreamland.

✳   ✳   ✳

Chapter 16: An Eco-system

When the four travelers awoke, many hours later, they discovered their next problem. White, fuzzy mold was all over their mushrooms.

"I've seen this before," Dem shared. "They're poison now."

Jin tasted one, just to be sure, but quickly spat it out, and didn't quit spitting for several minutes.

Tir frowned. "So much for our food supply, except for . . ." She pulled the rusty can of "Spinach" from the bottom of her bag. Everyone watched as she spent the next quarter hour carefully working with her mushroom knife to get the can open.

The gray-green slime that greeted them on the inside of the can caused their faces to twist.

"I see now," Dem began, "why the Tunnel Leaders weren't too careful about keeping *this* particular can locked up."

Tir pulled some of the greenish slime out with her fingers, tasted it, and pronounced it edible. They shared the contents equally in silence, but none of the four felt like they had just eaten a satisfying meal.

*

With bellies soon growling again, they continued to wander among the big stalagmites and stone draperies of the huge cavern, keeping as close to the right-hand wall as possible in the fading hope of seeing Bel and Fen again.

They slowly became aware that the wall was curving away from where they guessed the river was flowing. After another half hour of walking with slumped shoulders and heavy feet, they sat down on a dry flowstone and peered at the Map with glazed eyes.

"Farewell, friends," Tir whispered.

Tik nodded, remembering Fen, not very smart, but completely loyal to Bel.

After a few more minutes, Dem shook himself out of his sadness, which helped the others to do the same. "The Map only shows a small part of this big cavern. Somewhere on the other side should be a crawl-hole. I just hope there's only one."

"If we find one," Jin proposed, "we could keep going along the wall 'til we get back to the river beach, then we'll know for sure."

In the silence that lingered after Jin spoke, they suddenly heard three or four footsteps, on rocky ground, that quickly faded away.

Everyone remained silent and strained to hear more, but could only make out the faint sounds of their own breathing.

*

"I don't think that was a person," Dem whispered after several long minutes had passed.

"Something small, with hard feet," Tir speculated. "What were those called?"

"Hooves," Tik said softly in the silence.

"But . . ." Tir protested, "nothing with hooves has been *alive*, anywhere in the world, for *centuries!*"

Tik only shrugged.

*

Dem put away the Map and they began to wander through the cavern again, all four travelers pondering the sound of hooves on rock that had so briefly interrupted the silence.

Soon they came to a low place between cave formations where a little water and dirt had collected. They stood and stared, glow-stones held low, for out of the mud emerged tiny hoof prints that crossed a flowstone, then disappeared into broken rocks.

"Four-legged," Tir observed. "About the size of a . . . what were those things people used to have as pets?"

"Dogs," Jin began, "but they didn't have hooves."

Suddenly a tremendous noise of splashing, flapping, and shrill calls filled the cavern, and all four friends covered their ears. The sounds echoed off the walls, making the noise seem to come from everywhere at once.

Within a minute, the chaotic sounds died down. The travelers held their glow-stones high, but save for an occasional flash of something high in the air, they saw nothing.

Soon the shrill voices settled down into gentle cooing mixed with a flapping or splashing sound now and then.

"Cave birds!" Jin declared. "But *where* did they come from, and where's the *water* we heard, and what do they *eat?*"

With hunger beginning to gnaw at their empty stomachs, Jin's last question lingered in their minds. Tir decided to take the idea a step further. "And can we eat *them?*"

*

The four travelers resumed their wandering through the huge cavern, always staying fairly near the wall. Hope of seeing their missing friends faded from their minds as hunger asserted itself more and more painfully.

The cavern was no longer silent, as the sounds of birds cooing to each other, and occasionally taking flight, was now ever-present, although the splashing sound was rare. Seldom did the wanderers actually see the birds, and they all realized that Tir's idea for their next meal was probably not going to happen.

As they continued along the wall, some facts about the geometry of the cave began to penetrate their hunger-clouded minds. At the next halfway-comfortable place, Dem sat down, leaned against a rock, and looked up at the ceiling, still too high to be illuminated by their glow-stones. The others joined him.

"The birds are up there somewhere, probably nesting in cracks and ledges in the cavern ceiling, but we're never right under them, and we never see any droppings. I don't get it."

Everyone was silent for a minute, just listening to the cooing and flapping, never directly above them.

Suddenly Tik laughed.

The others looked at him.

"They must be in the middle. We've always stayed near the wall."

Dem grinned in the light of his glow-stone.

Tir and Jin looked at each other and smiled.

⁕

They had not gone far when they became painfully aware of why they had never pointed their feet toward the middle of the cavern, not counting their earlier desire to find another river beach. As soon as the wall was no longer in sight, they felt completely lost, and every direction looked exactly the same, save for the faint trail their own feet left in places.

Tir began breathing fast and her eyes became wide with fear. Dem noticed and took her hand.

Tik and Jin felt it enough to understand, but just flashed each other quick grins.

Tir was soon able to relax, but didn't let go of her brother's hand. The bird sounds were getting closer. Her curiosity, even if no dinner was forthcoming, made her go on.

⁕

The middle of the cavern nearly took their breath away. A roughly circular open area, perhaps forty feet across, sloped down to a deep pool of glowing water. The slopes around the pool were covered with bird droppings, and from those sprang mushrooms of many shapes and sizes.

Even as the four stood at the top of the slope with open mouths, the surface of the still water was broken by a bird who leapt into the air, spread its wings, and made for the ceiling above, dripping water onto the mushrooms below.

"That must be how the birds get in and out!" Jin proposed excitedly.

"Is light coming from that pool, or am I seeing things?" Tir asked.

Everyone pocketed their glow-stones.

Indeed, the pool cast a dim bluish-green light that allowed them to make out the nearest stalagmites and some of the larger mushrooms on the slope.

"Glow-stones in the pool?" Jin wondered aloud.

"Wrong color," Tik pointed out.

"Maybe ... something growing on the rocks underwater," Dem speculated.

Tik, still looking intently at the pool, nodded.

*

After a long silence to ponder all they could see, Tir spoke. "Not much chance of bird for dinner. How about some mushrooms?"

"I never thought I'd say this," Dem began, "but after going hungry for most of a day, the thought of more mushrooms isn't too bad."

Jin, only a beginning mushroom cutter back home, scrunched her face with worry. "But ... there are so many different *kinds* here! How do we know which ones are edible, and which poisonous?"

Tir, a planter who had been able to watch the sorters on many occasions, smiled. "I *think* I can help with that. And if nothing else, there's the old test that people have used for centuries."

The others looked at their mushroom expert.

She grinned for a second. "Eat mushrooms for dinner, go to sleep. If you wake up the next morning, the mushrooms were edible."

* * *

Chapter 17: Dinner

The four wanderers spent the next several hours carefully tiptoeing through the mushrooms that grew around the mysterious glowing pool. Tir looked at dozens of samples, sometimes knowing for sure they were edible. But at other times, she looked at them askance and carried the mushroom cap into the surrounding cave formations.

Dem and Tik seemed puzzled, but Jin understood.

Tir found a rock that was dark, if she was looking for light-colored spores in the mushroom, or a light rock if she wanted dark spores. She placed the mushroom cap with gills down, warned the boys not to touch, and returned to her task of looking over the fungus that might be their next nourishing meal if she did her job well, or their last meal if she didn't.

✳

By the time they had a respectable pile of edible mushrooms, and were thinking of sitting down to eat, Tir became aware that Jin, who was collecting fungus from the far side of the pool, was only bringing over good mushrooms.

"You learn fast, Jin," Tir declared. "You're now my assistant mushroom sorter!"

Jin laughed. "I can't take the credit. I'm just picking the kinds that our little friends with hooves eat." She brought over one with a bite out of it for the others to see.

After examining the new evidence, they all gathered around the pile of edible mushrooms.

Dem chewed with a thoughtful expression for several minutes, then spoke. "I wish we knew what has hooves and eats mushrooms. Maybe they could teach us a thing or two about this cavern."

"Probably hiding, until we're gone," Jin speculated.

✳

With bellies again full, bodies strengthening, and minds clearing, lighter topics of conversation arose.

"So the birds go out through the pool," Tir began, "eat whatever's outside, then come back and do their droppings in here, which feeds the mushrooms, and then there's something with hooves that eats the mushrooms, and adds more droppings."

"And now we're part of that eco-system, too!" Jin added.

Tik laughed, then wandered away into the stalagmites.

Dem swallowed a mouthful. "Now that we can think again, and have given up looking for Fen and Bel . . ."

A moment of sadness came over the group.

". . . I guess I should get out the Map and figure out where we're going," Dem finished.

"This cavern's so *big*," Tir began, "and now that we know it has food and water, it's easy to forget we were trying to do something."

Dem nodded as he pulled the Map from his bag. "I'm glad it's not paper, or it would be molding now, too."

Tik returned and sat down.

"We went the long way around," Dem observed, "because of looking for another river beach. The crawl-hole out of here should be most of the way back to our beach, if we keep going along the wall the way we were."

Tir took on a stern expression. "I think we should go *all* the way around, like Jin said, back to our beach. If we don't find the Angels, this cavern could be very important, since it has food."

Soon they were all yawning, so without a word, they got comfortable in a sandy area not far from the glowing pool. Tir's last statement echoed in their minds, and as they drifted into sleep, they all pondered the possibility of spending the rest of their lives in this and other caverns they might find, eating mushrooms, occasionally birds, and maybe even something with hooves . . .

✳

After everyone was awake, they set to work filling their bags with as many edible mushrooms as would fit, and keeping an extra to munch on while they walked. Dem led the way back toward the wall of the huge cavern. Luckily, their passage the first time, to explore the middle of the cavern, had left enough traces that the way was easy to find.

"Okay, we're looking for crawl-holes, or anything else important . . ." their leader began.

"Even if it's not the *right* crawl-hole," his sister pointed out, "we need to know about it."

"River beaches . . ." Jin muttered.

"Angels . . ." Tik whispered.

Dem nodded and pointed his feet along the cavern wall, in the direction they had originally been going.

✳

Again, the going was slow as the cave formations tended to cluster near the cavern walls. At first, nothing of interest revealed itself.

Most of an hour into their journey, Dem started frowning, and motioned for everyone to stop and be still. He listened intently, but finally shook his head in defeat.

They continued their journey.

Soon Dem stopped them again, and this time the sound lingered just a little too long to be one of them, or an echo.

"Hooves again?" Jin wondered aloud.

"But . . ." Tir began thoughtfully, "but not getting anywhere. More like . . . struggling."

Tik nodded agreement.

They walked on.

*

They might have walked right by the scene of the tragedy if a group of stalagmites hadn't force them away from the wall and right into a small, hidden hollow.

The guardian of the hollow, in his fear, might have done them great harm if he was larger.

As it was, he was only about a foot tall, and only with his head held high. Even so, the determination in his eyes made the four travelers stop and consider running for their lives.

They quickly got over their initial fright and looked over the situation. Two small deer-like creatures faced them. One, in the bottom of the hollow, stood on three legs, her fourth leg dangling uselessly at an odd angle. The other, on the far rim of the hollow, had his tiny legs planted firmly apart, and the look in his eyes told the travelers he would protect his mate with every fiber of his being, or die trying.

Tik smiled and strode forward, even though the male creature started stomping one tiny hoof in warning.

Tir and Jin both held their breath, thinking Tik was about to wring the little deer's neck and begin eating it, raw.

Tik was ready for the wounded female to fight him, but quickly discovered, as he took her in his arms, that no fight was left in her. Near exhaustion, she submitted to his hold as he carefully straightened the broken, twisted leg. She gave little painful cries while he worked, but then fell silent when her leg bones were all properly aligned.

The girls relaxed and breathed again.

The little male deer didn't relax, but ceased stomping the ground.

"I need . . . something stiff to wrap around it," Tik declared.

They quickly determined that Jin's mushroom bag was stiff, old canvas. Tik used it, and part of its shoulder strap, to make a splint for the little animal. The male guardian went back and forth from standing his ground on the edge of the hollow, to hiding behind the nearest stalagmite.

Jin, now possessing a pile of mushrooms but no bag, smiled to herself, placed a mushroom where she knew the male would soon return, and offered another to the female, still in Tik's arms.

Both little animals were soon eating, revealing that they had been dealing with their tragedy for many hours, if not days, and had had no time for anything else.

* * *

Chapter 18: New Traveling Companions

Not many minutes had passed when the four wanderers began to realize what they had gotten themselves into.

"Um . . . I wonder how long it will take for her leg to heal . . ." Jin said, looking at Tik.

He shrugged.

Dem, on the other hand, sighed. "Weeks."

Tir agreed with a single nod.

"Do we . . ." Jin began, but suddenly had to swallow several times. "Are there . . . enough mushrooms growing in this cavern . . . so we can wait that long?"

It was Tir's turn to sigh. "Not a chance. Just by filling our bags, we put a serious dent in that mushroom garden . . . at least, the edible part."

Dem frowned for a moment, then smiled. "That means . . . we'll have to take her with us! That will leave more mushrooms for the male deer. And you, Tik, will have to carry her!"

Tir looked at her brother and frowned, but didn't say anything.

Jin took a deep breath. "I just hope the Angels like deer."

✳

Tik gave Jin his bag so he could carry the little creature, and they otherwise made ready to continue their journey. Each person took several mushrooms from those that had been in Jin's old bag, and they munched as they walked.

Tir was still frowning as Dem began to lead along the cavern wall again. Even though *she* had not yet had a mate, she suddenly felt quite experienced in the matter . . . at least compared to her brother.

She burst out laughing, and was quickly joined by Jin, when Dem acted surprised that the little male deer was following close behind them.

"Did you *really* think we'd have only *one* deer joining us?" Tir asked, looking at her brother with a big grin.

He squirmed. "Oh . . . whatever. At least *he* can walk!"

Both girls laughed again. Tik just smiled.

*

Soon they came to the crawl-hole.

All four travelers frowned as they considered the tiny, jagged passageway that pierced the cavern wall. Even the deer seemed to be frowning.

"I *hope* that's the wrong crawl-hole," Tik said, looking down at the wounded animal in his arms, the same animal he would have to carry as he crawled and twisted his body through the narrow passageway.

Dem, still frowning, was pretty sure it was in just the right place to be the one. "Let's finish the circle and find out."

They continued along the wall of the cavern, around stalagmites, under stone draperies, across flowstones, and between boulders. Another half hour of travel brought them to the river beach, without any sign of another crawl-hole.

"Yep, it's our beach," Jin verified, looking at the footprints in the sand. "No Bel. No Fen. No other crawl-holes."

Tik growled.

Dem and Tir looked at each other.

The underground river flowed past smoothly, with just an occasional gurgle to break the silence.

*

Tik placed the little female on her feet at the edge of the river where the male was already drinking. She drank, then tried to take a step, but only cried in pain and began trembling. Tik soon picked her up and returned to the dry sand where he received a mushroom from Jin.

All six ate in silence, four of them remembering their lost companions.

Eventually Tik spoke. "I'll need lots of help with my little friend in that crawl-hole."

"You've got it!" Jin declared.

Tir smiled and nodded.

Dem was frowning as he gazed at the Map. "It looks like a *long* crawl-hole."

*

Less than an hour later, they peered at the jagged little hole again, the only way out of the cavern except the birds' pool and the river, either of which could mean death, neither of which would take them to the Angels' camp, according to the Map.

"Jin, will you scout the length of it?" Dem asked. "That way, Tik will be more prepared, and you can help from in front when he starts through."

"Sure! It doesn't look all that hard to me . . . I mean, me not carrying anything. What should I expect on the other side?"

"Medium-size tunnel, maybe a lava tube."

Jin nodded, adjusted the glow-stone protruding from her pocket, and quickly disappeared into the hole.

"I'll go behind Tik," Tir offered, "to help from that angle."

Dem nodded. "I go last, and help the male if he needs it."

*

"It's a meat grinder!" came Jin's voice from the crawl-hole. "But we can do it. Comes out in a smooth tunnel, old underground river, I think."

"Not like we have much choice . . ." Tik muttered. "We can do it, right little one?" he asked the small creature in his arms with a tender voice.

She made a sound that might have been a weak agreement, but didn't express confidence.

Tik took a couple of deep breaths before beginning his crawl.

Tir had been wrong. She didn't even have a chance to enter the crawl-hole after Tik, because the little male deer jumped in right behind him, and quickly showed that his little hooves were well-adapted to the situation.

*

A frustrating hour must have passed, which seemed like ten, as Tik crawled with one hand, and tried to keep the female deer from experiencing too much pain. Seldom could he move more than a few feet without needing to put her down, or pass her to Jin, while he navigated a tight place. Both situations caused her pain, but it quickly passed when she was once again in Tik's or Jin's arms.

Tir and Dem came behind, wishing they could be more helpful.

Finally, Jin exited the crawl-hole and slid down the smooth wall of the larger tunnel, then turned to receive the injured creature.

Tik slid down, felt sand under him, and sighed with relief.

The little male easily jumped down.

Tir slid next, and finally their leader. "Rest time!" Dem announced

"Heck, *nap* time!" Tik asserted and curled up on the sand, leaving others to deal with the injured deer for a while.

* * *

Chapter 19: The Trap

Tik only slept a couple of hours, then woke to find the other three eating mushrooms and looking at the Map. The injured female deer, lying in the sand next to the male, became excited and tried to stand when she saw Tik get up, but only cried in pain.

"You have an admirer!" Jin teased.

"After what I put her through in that crawl-hole, I'm surprised."

Tir smiled and Dem chuckled.

"If you're done napping," Dem began, glancing at the tall boy stretching himself awake, "we need to go *that* way," he continued, pointing, "and look for a ledge on the right side."

Tik looked. The tunnel, only two or three strides across, sloped downward slightly in that direction. The walls, as far as he could see, continued to be the same smooth, pale rock he had slid down earlier, with sand covering the floor. "What's in the other direction?"

"Just sand," Jin revealed, "until it ends in a vertical shaft that goes up, unclimbable, not too far from here."

"Mushroom?" Tir offered.

※

Dem was convinced that the Map was not to scale, but even so, he explained, it appeared that the sandy tunnel was quite long.

No one minded, although Tir pointed out that their food supply would only last another day, two if they skimped. All four travelers knew they were walking away from the only known mushroom patch and into the unknown, but couldn't think of any good alternative.

The little female was content as long as she was being carried. The male was happy walking close beside Tik.

※

The minutes stretch into hours. The tunnel, clearly once an underground river, coursed almost perfectly straight, and always slightly downhill. The wanderers took turns leading, and both Dem and Tir carried the little injured deer for a time to let Tik stretch his arms.

Jin was leading when several things happened at once.

The tunnel began to slope down much more steeply, so steeply that the bare smooth rock on the floor was exposed.

Dem was carrying the little deer, and hadn't been thinking about the ledge they needed to find.

Tir was walking on Dem's right, chatting about funny things that used to happen in the mushroom-growing caves.

The male deer walked along between them.

Tik came last, trying to shake the kinks out of his sore arms.

Suddenly the little male animal felt the bare rock under his hooves, stopped in his tracks, and made an urgent sound that got everyone's attention.

Dem stopped only a pace farther along and glimpsed the ledge on the right wall of the cave. "I think this is where we turn off!"

Jin, several paces ahead, swiveled to see what was happening, but with smooth rock sloping down, and a little dry sand to lubricate it, her shoes keep moving forward. "I . . . I can't . . . I can't stop!"

She flopped to her belly to use her hands, but they found little more traction than her feet.

Tir managed to stop as she too spotted the ledge and realized what was happening to Jin.

Tik felt mortal fear and dread rise up inside him. He watched helplessly from behind the group as Jin disappeared down the smooth rock slope into the darkness below.

✳

For several endless seconds, silence filled the tunnel.

Dem had to swallow several times before he could make any sound. "J . . . Jin?"

From the darkness ahead came a voice. "I'm okay. It's just a pit . . . maybe . . . fifteen feet deep, and the floor is soft sand."

Those above breathed deep sighs of relief.

"No one go any closer to the slippery slope!" Dem ordered. "We'll use the ledge to see Jin."

All three, and the little male deer, carefully backed up until they were once again on sand that stayed in place. Tir held her glow-stone up to examine the ledge. "Not too hard."

"I can't see you!" Jin's voice said from the dark pit with a hint of anxiety. "What're you guys doing?"

"Checking out the ledge!" Dem called down. "Looks like we can cross it, and once we're part-way across, we'll be able to see you and figure out how to get you out!"

"I have small but easy tunnels going off in two directions!" Jin called up in a more relaxed tone. "No idea where they go."

"I don't think they're on the Map!" Dem said from memory, handing the little female to Tik. "I'm starting across!"

Dem took the crossing of the ledge slowly, had little trouble, and was soon able to see Jin in the pit below. He could also see one of the smaller tunnels she had mentioned. He frowned when he got far enough to realize that all the walls of Jin's pit were the same smooth rock. He forced himself to look at something else. "Just one little place on the ledge, Tir and Tik, where it's narrow and you have to be super-careful."

"We see it," Tir assured him. "Tik's starting across with the little one. I wonder if I should carry . . ."

Her thought was cut off as the male deer leapt onto the ledge and easily stayed right at Tik's heels.

"Never mind," Tir said with a smile.

Everyone was soon past the narrow place on the ledge. They all noticed that their tunnel, on the far side, also sloped down into the pit, and once there, they would again be unable to see their friend in the pit below.

"Hi, up there!" Jin called.

"Hi, down there!" Tir responded, smiling.

"Any cracks in the rock you can use to climb up?" Dem asked.

"Not yet . . . still looking," she relied, holding her glow-stone high as she examined the walls.

As soon as Tik made the injured female comfortable in the sand on the far side, and the male planted himself beside her, the three friends returned to the ledge. Near the middle, they sat down to consider the situation.

"Do NOT jump or slide into the pit, any of you!" Jin commanded. "You know me, I don't need much to call it a handhold or foothold. But . . . I'm not finding any. You *sure* this lower level isn't on the Map, Dem?"

He pulled it out to check his memory. "The pit and ledge are — the pit's just a dark circle, not labeled — but no hint of your lower tunnels. We're supposed to keep going on this level after crossing the ledge."

Jin sighed.

"Don't worry, Jin, we're not leaving you behind!" Tir asserted.

Jin sighed again. "You might have to," she said softly.

For the next three hours, Jin made every possible effort to climb the walls of her prison — and some efforts that could only be called super-human.

During the fourth hour, she attempted to pile up sand to make herself a ramp. She was small, but her weight caused the loose, dry sand to flatten back out, save for an inch or two for her hour of work.

They had no rope, and were well-aware that probably none, of sufficient strength, remained in the world after so many centuries.

During the fifth hour, Tir demanded all three coats from those on the ledge, and tired the arms together. On the eighth try, Jin was able to run and leap high enough to catch the end of the make-shift rope, but Dem's coat tore right in half, and the other two showed signs that they would have, if Dem's hadn't.

After pulling up the remaining two and a half coats, Tir gave hers to Dem, then started crying.

*

Tik, who had helped with everything they tried, had remained completely silent during the entire six-hour ordeal. Finally, he went to check on the deer.

By this time, Jin had become completely silent also, sifting sand through her fingers where she sat in the middle of her pit-prison.

Soon Tik returned to the ledge. "Both deer are getting very hungry."

"We all are," Dem assured him. "I'll give them something from my bag in a minute."

Tik nodded. "I've been thinking, and now I've decided, so don't try to stop me. I've fathered three children with girls I didn't even like so this pathetic little dying civilization of ours could go on a little longer."

Tir looked at him with wide eyes from where she perched on the ledge.

"Now, I actually *like* a girl," Tik went on, "and I'm NOT going to leave her to die alone in some strange tunnels she can't get out of."

Dem swallowed, guessing what Tik was about to do. He wished he could think of a good reason to talk his friend out of it, but none came to mind.

"You guys have all the mushrooms that are . . . you know . . . on this level," Tik continued in a soft voice. "Please take care of the little ones for me."

Having spoken, Tik stepped over Dem and Tir, crept along the ledge back to the main tunnel, then slid down the same smooth rock slope that Jin had slid down six hours before.

* * *

Chapter 20: Joining and Parting

Tik and Jin stood looking at each other in silence for several minutes. Dem and Tir, on the ledge, were also silent. The soft sounds made by the two deer, where they lay together in the sand, could be clearly heard.

Finally Jin swallowed. "Wow ..." she softly intoned. "Want a ... mushroom?"

Tik smiled and nodded, then looked up toward the ledge. "Me and Jin have some tunnels to explore. You guys have some Angels to find. If we don't see you again ... be happy. I trust you'll know what to do with the deer. Maybe that leg will heal enough so they can go off on their own again ... I don't know."

Tir was silently crying. "We'll ... take good care of them, I promise."

Dem could also feel moisture gathering in his eyes. "You guys be happy, too."

Tik accepted a mushroom from Jin, offered her his hand, and together they disappeared into one of the small tunnels that led out of the bottom level of the pit.

✳

A few minutes later, Dem and Tir both realized they were sitting on a ledge looking into an empty, silent pit.

"Time to give the little ones something to eat," Tir said as she got up.

"And us, too," Dem added.

Tir chuckled as she wiped her tears onto her sleeve and started working her way along the ledge.

Once they were seated on the sand near the deer and everyone was eating, Tir took a hard look inside her mushroom bag, and glanced at Dem's. "With feeding the deer, about a day."

Dem was silent for a long moment as he looked into his bag. "At the most."

They both ate quietly for another minute.

"I guess . . ." Dem began, gathering his thoughts, ". . . you and me started this journey . . . and you and me were meant to finish it, just a brother and sister."

"How does that fit with your dream?" she asked, looking at him with her head slightly cocked.

Dem looked at the sand and remained silent for a long moment. "It's . . . exactly what happened in the dream . . . but I was . . . too embarrassed to tell you before."

Tir smiled at her brother, although he didn't see it, and then decided it was a good time to change the subject a little. "Well . . . we *know* Fim and Tol won't be finishing the journey with us, and Bel, Fen, Jin, and Tik aren't on the right path . . . at least, according to the Map . . . but we still have no idea if *we* can finish it."

Dem looked up. "I guess . . . there's nothing to do but try."

"Yeah."

*

Without discussing it, they both knew this was the point of no return. From the area of the pit, they could get back to the mushroom patch in the big cavern before starving to death.

They both looked in that direction for a moment, then turned and considered the unknown darkness ahead. The tunnel appeared to slope slightly upward away from the pit.

"Water must have come from both directions," Dem thought aloud, "and drained into the pit."

Tir nodded. "Maybe Jin and Tik will find out where it once went, and there will be birds, and mushrooms, and maybe even deer, just like in the big cavern!"

"Maybe," he said as he shrugged out of Tir's old coat and handed it to her. "I *know* I'm going to stay warm carrying the little one and walking uphill."

She hesitated, then accepted the coat. "Okay, but it goes over *both* of us when we're sleeping."

"Agreed," he said, picked up the little female animal, and side by side with his sister, began the next leg of their journey.

*   *   *

Chapter 21: Going Up

Two hours later, Tir stood looking up at the smooth rock walls all around them and sighed. "I should have guessed. Exactly the same as the other end."

Both deer were also looking up, one from Dem's arms, the other from the sandy floor.

"Ummm . . ." Dem intoned thoughtfully after slowly turning a complete circle, ". . . not *exactly* the same. That broken edge up there is only about eight feet up."

Tir frowned. "Okay, so you'll give me a boost up . . . then what?"

Dem set down the little female and held his glow-stone over his head. "Hmmm. Then . . . you'll pull *me* up!"

Tir frowned even more deeply. "O . . . kay . . ."

*

After a mushroom for courage, Tir realized that her shoes wouldn't really help with the climb, and would probably hurt Dem's shoulders, so she took them off. "You can toss them to me once I'm up."

Dem nodded.

The two deer watched as Tir first stepped into Dem's clasped hands, then up to his shoulders. From her wobbly perch, only the nearby wall kept her from falling.

"Okay," Tir called from above, "I can get my arms over the edge."

Dem couldn't see anything. "Now you have to hold yourself up so I can switch to pushing on your feet."

"There's not much to . . . hold onto . . . maybe this little . . . crack in the rock. There."

Dem felt Tir become lighter, so he changed positions quickly and pushed. "Climb!"

She scrambled for anything she could grab, causing several small rocks to rain down on Dem and the deer. Finally, her upper half was over the edge, her feet now out of Dem's reach. "Sorry about the junk," she gasped out.

Dem glanced at the deer. "We're okay."

Tir pulled her legs over the edge, sat up, and got out her glow-stone to examine her new environment.

*

"Wow . . ." she breathed.

"What?"

"Stalagmites . . . flowstones . . . old water channels . . . big, but not as big as the bird cavern."

"That matches the Map," Dem said from below. "Shoes coming up!"

Tir giggled as they landed nearby.

Getting the deer to the upper level was not so easy. Held as high as Dem could reach, the little female cried in pain. Tir lay on her belly and stretched her arms down as far as she could. She feared she would over-balance and fall, but was able to get her hands around the deer's middle. Dem continued to help by pushing on the little animal's dangling hooves, avoiding the injured leg.

Finally, Tir and the little female flopped onto the rocks and both gasped for breath.

"Sorry it's not soft sand, little one," Tir said in a comforting tone.

*

The male deer was a different kind of problem. He had never before needed any help, and indeed had never let any of the humans touch him.

But now his mate was eight feet up, and he had no way of crossing that gulf by himself.

He strutted this way and that, tried to climb the walls under his own power, and ran back down the tunnel a few yards before returning.

Both Tir, above, and Dem, on his level, weren't sure whether to laugh or cry. They understood what he was going through, but couldn't think of any way to help that didn't involve touching him.

The little male creature made heart-rending sounds that expressed his frustration.

"What're we gonna do?" Tir asked from above.

Dem sat down and pulled a mushroom from his bag. "Just wait, I guess."

Tir sighed, and got out mushrooms for herself and the little female.

*

An hour later, fighting every instinct in his mind and body, the little male hung his head in front of Dem.

"I think he's as ready as he'll ever be," Dem called up to his sister. "Get ready for one scared critter in your arms."

"Oh, joy."

As soon as Dem picked him up, the male's little legs started moving, but Dem ignored them, and the resulting scratches on his arms, as he hoisted the animal up.

"Poor thing, he's so scared ..." Tir said in comforting tones as she reached, grabbed, and pulled.

The male was running toward his mate almost before Tir could put him down. She couldn't suppress a chuckle.

Then she remembered her brother and looked down. "You okay?"

"Yeah, just a few hoof-scratches. I should have been wearing the coat. Didn't think of it."

"Me neither. Sorry."

*

Dem rested, ate another mushroom, then tossed his bag and glow-stone up to his sister. "Okay, that's everything . . . except me."

Brother and sister pondered the situation in silence for a few minutes. Dem could reach up about six feet. From her belly, Tir could reach down almost two feet. A leap would add a little. Dem took the next quarter hour to pile up as much sand as possible.

As life-long cave dwellers, they knew that clasping hands would do no good. Their only hope was to get ahold of each other's wrists.

Dem took several deep breaths, than sprang. Their hands and wrists met.

Tir screamed in pain as her ribs were crushed against the rock beneath her.

Dem scrambled with his feet for *anything* that would allow him to get higher.

Tir ignored her pain and pulled with all her might.

Dem found nothing that gave him any traction.

As much as she wanted to find the strength to pull her bother up, it was nowhere to be found in her slender arms.

They both stayed in that painful, frustrating place a moment longer, then let go.

Dem fell onto the sand and gasped for air.

Tir's mind filled with the pain from her ribs, arms, and hands, and she began crying deeply, right where she lay.

*

After her tears had run their course, Tir was still lying on her belly, her mind numb and her body sore, when a wet nose touched her cheek. She turned her head slightly to find the male deer looking at her.

"Yes, little one, we're in a pickle. Dem's down there, I'm up here, and your sweetheart has a broken leg. Pickles all around."

The little deer made a sound in his throat.

"I'm open to suggestions, but you'll have to explain your idea a little more . . ."

Tir suddenly quit speaking, and her mouth hung open. She propped herself onto her sore elbows and looked down. Her brother was sitting up now, dealing silently with his own frustrations.

"Guess what I just realized!" Tir called down.

After sniffling once, Dem looked up. "What?"

"We can do this! We just need to put the one with strong arms at the top, because that's where they'll be needed, and the one who weighs less at the bottom!"

Dem thought for a moment. "But . . . that's the exact opposite of where we are!"

Tir made her favorite rude noise.

Dem smiled, but it soon changed to a frown. "That means I'd have to stand on your shoulders."

"I can handle that. And I might not be able to *push* you up like you did for me, but I can make footholds against the wall with my hands, and you can *pull* yourself up!"

Dem thought about it, then grinned up at his very smart sister.

Tir swung her legs over the edge, hung from her hands, then let go and dropped to the sand below. Dem steadied her when she landed.

The male deer looked down from the edge as if the silly human female had just lost her mind.

Tir started wondering the same thing when she felt Dem's weight in her clasped hands. She was sure of it when he went to her shoulders. "Ouch! Don't stay there any longer than you have to!"

"I promise!" He reached over the edge and felt for the crack his sister had used. "That better?"

"Much. Now hold on while I support your . . . right foot. Unless you prefer the left."

"Don't care. Okay, here goes."

She pushed, or at least tried to keep his foot in the same place, and he pulled with all his might. The effort caused him to roar like a lion, even though he only knew of lions from picture books. The male deer jumped back in fright and stood guard over the female.

When Dem had most of his weight on the upper level, he fell silent and looked up. "Sorry," he said to the frightened little animals.

"I *think* that was the hard part," Dem said, receiving his shoes as Tir tossed them up.

"I'm *sure* it was for my shoulders!"

Dem frowned. "The next part isn't going to be nice to your shoulders, either."

Tir sighed. "Just give me a few minutes," she said, swinging her arms, "then I really don't care what happens, as long as I'm up there. Here comes my glow-stone."

"Got it."

Tir took several more minutes to feel ready, all the time flexing and stretching her arms and shoulders. While pacing, she mentally took stock of their possessions — one coat, two glow-stones, two nearly-empty mushroom bags, and four old shoes. Everything was at the top, waiting for her.

"I'm ready," she declared. "You?"

Dem was swinging his arms too. "If we aren't ready soon, we'll starve to death, right here."

Tir chuckled. "That's motivation, if anything is. Here I come, ready or not!"

Dem got down on his belly. He received Tir's wrists, and this time roared like a dragon, which he had not seen in picture books but thought it probably roared even louder than a lion. He pulled with all his strength and hope, going up to his knees in the process, while Tir did her part by bending her arms and scrambling to get her feet over the edge.

They collapsed together onto the rocky floor of the upper cavern and just breathed. Both their bodies screamed at them with pain, which they completely ignored.

After getting over the fright caused by the dragon-roar, the two deer looked at the two humans with deepened respect.

✳ ✳ ✳

Chapter 22: The Twisted Cavern

Dem and Tir awoke from painful dreams several hours later in the same place they had collapsed — on the rocky floor of a large cavern, close to an eight foot drop that had taken all their strength and determination to climb.

They awoke with arms and legs tangled, and spent several minutes muttering apologies as they untangled themselves.

Two small deer paused in licking each other's fur to glance at the humans, then returned to their grooming.

Eventually, Dem and Tir collected their wits enough to sit up and consider their situation. Tir looked in her mushroom bag, found two, and handed them to the deer.

Dem found one and a half in his bag, which he divided equally between himself and his sister. "That's it."

"Hear that, guys?" Tir said to the small animals still eating their mushrooms. "What you see is what you get."

"Maybe this is another bird cavern," Dem wondered aloud.

They both fell silent for a moment to listen for bird sounds, but heard nothing.

After finishing his mushroom pieces, Dem pulled the remaining item from his bag. "According to the Map . . . we're in a medium-size cavern with an exit tunnel somewhere on the far side."

They took a moment to look around, as far as their glow-stones would illuminate. Old waterways seemed to twist every which way on the cavern floor, and once came together in their current location before plunging into the tunnel below. More recently, stalagmites and flowstones had covered some of the old water channels, and stone draperies and stalactites had grown down from the ceiling.

"After this cavern," Dem continued, looking at the Map again, "there's just a short little tunnel, then the cavern where the Angels . . . camp? Float around on shafts of pure energy? Whatever."

Tir looked up from the Map, grinning.

With a little strength spreading from his belly to his sore muscles, Dem stood up and stretched his arms. "I guess we'd better get started."

Tir shouldered her empty mushroom bag. "Your turn to wear the coat."

He nodded as he put it on and picked up the little female animal, but fully intended to give the coat back to his sister as soon as he got warmed up from walking.

✳

During the next three hours, with his last burst of energy rapidly fading, Dem led his sister along seven different ancient water channels, all of which ended in unclimbable vertical shafts, or looped back to another dry channel in the same cavern. None required crawling, so the little deer in his arms experienced no pain. The male followed along behind faithfully. As the hours passed, Dem began moaning with frustration, and stumbling on loose rocks more and more often.

After a short rest, he took another two hours to drag himself and his little company into four crawl-holes, but none went anywhere. During those hours, at first Tir could see him holding back tears, then later not bothering to hold them back as they ran out of crawl-holes to explore.

Back in the complex cavern with its many dry water channels, Dem plopped down onto a rock and finally poured out his feelings. "I don't understand it. I keep trying things, and they don't go anywhere! But one of them has to! It just has to . . ." He wilted into deep sobs.

Tir sat down close beside him and put an arm around his shoulders. He was still wearing their only coat, but she didn't say a word.

The two deer, sitting together on another rock, looked at the two humans with dark, sympathetic eyes.

✳

Another half hour passed as Dem mumbled his sadness and anger at his dying civilization, at every rock in every tunnel and cavern in the world, and at himself. He admitted that his head was pounding and he couldn't think straight.

His sister listened and nodded agreement at everything he said. She was experiencing all the same feelings, and was as close to starvation as him, but somehow she knew that only one of them could be weak at a time, and it was his turn.

So Tir, nine-year-old mushroom planter of Sonmatia Two, looked inside herself for the courage to be the strong one. She knew she didn't need it for very long — they would either find food and water soon, or die.

Her brother continued to cry softly and mutter his frustrations, and the two little deer curled up together to sleep.

✳

"I have an idea."

Almost a minute passed before Dem realized that his sister had said something important.

"Wha . . . what?"

Tir took a deep breath. "There are *lots* of tunnels and crawl-holes out of this cavern, right?"

"Uh huh. And we've tried them all, some of them twice."

"How do we *know* we've tried them all?"

Dem's head was pounding worse than ever before, and he couldn't think of an answer.

In the silence, Tir continued. "We're going to try them all again, and make a pile of rocks at the entrance to each one. If there's any we missed, we'll find it. We'll leave the deer here *until* we find it." She resisted the temptation to also suggest that her brother wait with the deer.

Dem sat blinking and trying to think, but only succeeded at blinking.

Tir stood up. "You with me?"

Dem swallowed, and with a great effort, stood, but couldn't think of anything to say.

❋

Once again, sister and brother again dragged themselves into and out of tunnels and crawl-holes. They had lost all ability to guess the passing of time. It may have taken two hours, or six. They didn't know nor care. It was their last effort.

Making little piles of rocks took all the strength left in their arms. Putting one foot in front of the other drained their legs. Slowly, hardly realizing it, they started running out of tunnels without rock markers.

Breathing became hard, but they didn't sense the air was bad, just that they were exhausted beyond anything they had ever experienced.

"That's all of them . . . I think," Dem gasped out, hands on his knees. "They all . . . have markers."

"Now we find . . . the one that doesn't," Tir said, also struggling to breath.

Dem nodded. He had no hope of succeeding. It was just something to pass the time before dying.

❋

They stumbled this way and that on the edge of the cavern, sometimes leaning on each other, sometimes falling onto a rock to rest, or perhaps just die, they were never quite sure which. They found all the half-remembered tunnel and crawl-hole entrances, each with it's rock marker.

Finally Tir collapsed onto an angled boulder and leaned back. She gazed up at the cavern wall in front of her. A stalagmite was casting a dark shadow on the wall.

Why is that shadow so dark?

She struggled to wrap her mind around the situation, but the pounding in her head made it difficult. She looked around, and saw that Dem was about five feet to her right.

Even if my glow-stone's casting a shadow, Dem's should be lighting up the wall behind the stalagmite.

Her eyes snapped open wider. "Dem, we just looked for tunnels at about the level of the cavern floor, right?"

He blinked several time. "We looked up at the walls and ceiling plenty of times, and didn't see . . ."

Tir looked at her brother. He was looking in the right direction, and his eyes were open wide. "You see it?" she asked.

He struggled to stand up, then moved his glow-stone back and forth while he watched the shadow behind the stalagmite.

Tir watched also. "It think . . . it always looked like a shadow, so we didn't really see it. Is it in the right place on the Map?"

With weak and trembling hands, Dem struggled to unfold the Map. A long moment of silence passed.

Tir looked from the Map to the cavern wall several times and knew the answer even before Dem spoke.

"Yes . . ." he whispered with trembling lips.

✳   ✳   ✳

Chapter 23: Angels

The deer were amazed when the two humans returned, laughing and talking and acting as if they had just had a nutritious meal and a good night's sleep. And yet, there remained a hollow look in the humans' eyes, especially the boys'. Also, no mushrooms, or anything else to eat, was being offered, and the deer knew these humans would share any food they had.

Dem realized that he had been wearing their only coat for a long time, and handed it to Tir with guilty looks. "Sorry. I guess I sort of lost it there for a while. You're the leader now. You did the thinking . . . and looking . . . that got us out of this mess."

Tir smiled slightly. "Maybe you should hold that thought until we know if the shadow-tunnel *goes* anywhere."

"If it doesn't . . ." Dem left his sentence unfinished.

Tir nodded as she put on the coat.

⁕

The shadowy tunnel was about four feet up the cavern wall, but some nearby rocks, and the stalagmite that had hidden it, gave footholds. Tir went first, held her glow-stone up, and announced that the way appeared to be passable, and not too difficult. Dem handed the injured deer up to his sister.

They had to hunch over most of the way, and crawl for a short distance, but soon came to the next cavern, the cavern that should, according to the Map, include the Angels' camp.

As the tunnel opening was about two feet off the cavern floor on that end, they sat down on the edge to see what they could see. Their glow-stones faintly illuminated a few nearby cave formations, as always, but a light of a different color — a warmer color — penetrated their awareness from somewhere far across the cavern. Both deer were also looking in that direction.

"Let's put away our glow-stones," Tir whispered.

Slowly, with the lights hidden, their eyes adjusted.

Tir squinted and forced herself to think. "That's the wrong color to be even the brightest glow-stones, and it's not like the glowing mushroom pool, either. Could that be . . . sunlight from outside?"

Dem was the only one who had glimpsed daylight through the few windows in the Government Tunnels where he used to work. "No. That light's a sickly yellow because of the bad air. This is . . . whiter . . . softer and nicer somehow. Shall we go meet the Angels?"

Tir looked at the ground. "Dem, there's something I want to talk to you about first, something that I think we might have to do . . . especially because we lost all the others who came with us . . . and I want you to know that . . . if we have to . . . it'll be okay with me . . ."

Dem and Tir of Sonmatia Two talked for another quarter hour, but hunger and exhaustion, temporarily forgotten, began to reassert themselves. The travelers still had a large cavern to cross before, hopefully, they could beg for something to eat and drink.

The four moved slowly across the cavern as if in a dream. Three, with sore legs and empty bellies, staggered forward, no one leading, just always moving toward the warm white light. The fourth one, equally hungry, dozed in Dem's arms, putting complete trust in the humans who had saved her from certain death.

They didn't try to hurry, as they were very close to falling down at any moment, and they knew it. Also, they sensed that a very important time in their lives was coming to an end, and a deep instinct made them want to savor its final moments.

They didn't realize how close to the Angels' camp they were until a tall girl with long silver hair stood before them, and behind her, from just over a slight rise, came the warm glow of the Angels' lights.

"Greetings! I am Feli-tala Rima, and I am the language specialist for Sonmatia Two — your planet — on the life-monitor ship Tirilana Kril. We have been waiting for you."

Somewhat to Dem surprise, the little male deer walked over to the tall girl and nuzzled her leg.

She knelt down and stroked the animal. "Hello, little friend. Are you and Pama well?"

Even though no words or sounds were exchanged that Tir or Dem could hear, a moment later the tall girl frowned. "I'm sorry. We'll get that fixed right away."

She stood back up. "We have some food and drink at the camp, if you tired travelers can walk just a little farther . . ."

Dem could feel Tir standing close beside him, so he gathered his courage and cleared his throat. "Um . . . we have something we need to say. We know you want us to go to another world and . . . um . . . restart our civilization there. We tried to bring a bunch of other people with us who . . . you know . . . wanted to be mates. But we lost them all along the way."

The silver-haired girl nodded with understanding, but didn't interrupt.

"The problem is . . . you see . . . me and Tir are brother and sister, and we know it's not the best thing for the gene pool for a brother and sister to be mates . . . but if it's absolutely necessary . . . we'll do it."

The tall girl smiled slightly. "Your intimate relationship with each other is your own business, but I have two things to reveal to you."

Dem and Tir both looked at her with as much curiosity as their exhaustion and hunger would allow.

"First of all, we seem to have plenty of mated pairs from your world already. Please, come to the camp and see."

✳

The golden ship, a perfect sphere with an open hatch on the side, perched on three legs in a clear area between several large stalagmites. From it, beams of soft light splashed upon the cavern ceiling above, casting a gentle glow over the entire camp and surrounding area.

The wide sandy area in front of the ship contained several tables of different heights, some with stools. At one table, two people and a large bird sat playing some kind of game.

Tir's throbbing mind took a moment to recognize the people, but when she did, she nearly screamed. "Bel! It's Bel and Fen! They're alive!" She tried to dash forward, but tripped on a rock.

Feli-tala Rima caught her. "Take it slowly. Yes, your friends are alive and well."

Bel and Fen hopped up and dashed to greet the new arrivals. Feli-tala offered to take the female deer from Dem, and then she and the large bird stood aside while the four friends embraced.

"We tried so hard to find you guys!" Dem explained.

Fen brushed the concern away with his hand. "Don't worry about it! It would have been impossible, until now."

They all moved down to the tables. The bird waddled up the ramp and into the ship.

"The river spat us out onto a sandy beach not much after we last saw you," Bel said, "and a long, winding tunnel brought us here!"

Pitchers of water and fruit juice were placed on the table by Tik, and Jin set down a tray with several cups. Both were grinning from ear to ear as they sat down.

Dem and Tir clasped hands and arms with the friends they thought would be dying of starvation in the lower tunnels. Soon they remembered their hunger and thirst, and took a moment to drink deeply, starting with the cold, delicious water.

"We just followed our feet," Jin said with a smile, "and soon found ourselves in *this* cavern, with that beautiful warm light to guide us."

Tik, also smiling, nodded.

Before any more words could be exchanged, Ril and Bim came down the ramp with plates of fruit and nuts.

Tir stood and hugged the large girl. "I thought you'd be working double-shifts in the mushroom caves for the rest of your life!"

"I would have been," Ril confirmed, "so why not tell everyone what I was thinking?"

"And she did, and they listened!" Bim added proudly.

"And the next day, *seventeen* pairs met us at the exit cave!"

"And Ril was *so* brave, going down that tight climb-hole again!"

"And when we came to the first Outer Patrol, they looked at the thirty-six people in front of them." Ril paused and grinned. "Then they said, 'You're all under arrest.' And you know what happened next?"

Tir and Dem remained silent, but were smiling.

"We laughed!" Bim announced. "I'm sure Ril started it, but a second later, all of us were laughing our heads off!"

At that moment, the other seventeen couples came pouring out of the ship. Tir and Dem recognized most of them. They gathered around the table and mumbled thanks to the brother and sister who had made their freedom possible.

"Feli-tala met us just a little ways up that large lava tube, the one with Outer Patrols," Ril explained, "and then showed us a short-cut, so we had a *much* easier trip than you guys."

Dem and Tir nodded and continued to listen, but absolutely had to start munching on fruit and nuts.

"Sorry we don't have any mushrooms," Bim said with a straight face.

"That's okay," Tir assured him, smiling, as she slipped a slice of fruit into her mouth, the first she had ever tasted.

✳

"And we can have as many babies as we want!" Ril exclaimed.

Tir didn't relate to that idea, but tried not to let it show on her face.

"Or as few as we want, or even none!" another girl said with just as much excitement.

The boy at her side looked a little disappointed.

"And girls get as much say in mating as boys do," Jin said sternly.

Tir noticed that she and Tik were still sitting close together.

"And we can wait until we feel *ready*," a young boy added, "instead of having older boys taunt us until we do it."

Dem nodded with understanding.

"And we'll live fifty years or more!" another boy said excitedly, "as long as we don't fall out of a tree . . . whatever that is."

Dem chuckled, but had just as little experience with trees.

"So we can actually *raise* our children!" Bel added, "instead of *dying* before they can even walk."

Tir smiled at the thought, but her expression quickly change to a frown. "How's Sim, the planting supervisor?"

Everyone fell silent. Ril shook her head.

"Population should be about two forty and dropping," a boy said. "Feli-tala thinks another group might be working up the courage to defy the Tunnel Thugs and get out."

"So the people of our new world," a girl speculated, "will be the strong ones with enough courage to think for themselves, not the control freaks and those who hide behind them."

Feli-tala Rima, at the far end of the table, had been silent while the young people of Sonmatia Two shared recent news. Now she spoke. "Your civilization has been in grave danger for many years. It will take a new world, lots of support from us, and several generations to get you out of danger. And yes, lots of courage and thinking for yourselves."

Dem had a thoughtful look on his face. Tir and several others noticed and looked at him.

He turned to Feli-tala Rima. "Why did you even bother talking to the Tunnel Thugs — I mean the government?"

The tall girl with silver hair smiled. "Just out of respect. Theoretically, they are supposed to represent your interests."

Many of the assembled people of Sonmatia Two snickered.

"They represent their own bellies and their ... um ... mating preferences," a girl said boldly.

The snickering grew louder.

Feli-tala continued smiling. "We knew it wouldn't do any good, but it's a step we had to take. No mortal government, anywhere in the local universe, has ever faithfully represented its people. If one ever did, everyone in Nebador would just faint with surprise . . ."

All of the assembled citizens of Sonmatia Two, from ages seven to fourteen, laughed deeply and couldn't regain their composure for a long time.

✳

"And we also have the requirement," Feli-tala Rima continued once the laughter had died down, "that those who want to leave must clearly demonstrate that desire. That's why we waited until you had made a journey, although the length and difficulty of the journey Tir and Dem took, had a different purpose."

Everyone looked at the silver-haired girl, sensing something important was about to happen.

"This is the other thing I promised to reveal to you, Tir and Dem. You can go with the other brave people of your civilization to a new world, if you want, and raise families there, or not, as you choose. But also, I wish to extend to you an invitation to follow a different path. I know of the many challenges and hardships you faced on your journey, challenges that would have crushed most people. You may, if you wish, come with us, after we take your friends to their new world, and join us in doing the work of the gods."

Suddenly, all the other assembled citizens of Sonmatia Two began clapping and grinning at the brother and sister.

Dem's throat was too dry to speak. He felt his sister take his hand under the table.

Tir found her voice first, and spoke with wide eyes of wonder. "You mean . . . become Angels?"

Feli-tala smiled. "I think *angels' helpers* would be a better term."

"What . . . what would we do?" Dem managed to ask. "We don't know anything but recycling trash and planting mushrooms."

The others chuckled or smiled with understanding.

Feli-tala answered. "There are many possibilities, and you would be free to choose, but I might suggest you start with Stewardship while you learn everything else you need to know. Your skills of recycling and planting are a good start, and you would add to that a broad understanding of biology, ecology, and climatology, until you are able to help with the management of whole ecosystems in star stations, and eventually on natural planets themselves."

"Wow . . ." Tir breathed. "That . . . sounds like . . . a lot more fun than planting mushrooms!"

Dem nodded agreement. "Can we . . . you know . . . visit our friends on their new world?"

"Yes. They will grow under the direct care of the gods and angels for many years, until someday they are strong enough to follow their own destinies."

"And . . . can . . ." Tir began with hesitation, "Dem and me . . . stay close? I mean . . . we don't want to be mates, but we still like each other a lot . . . especially after that *journey!*"

Dem verified with a vigorous nod.

Feli-tala Rima smiled again. "You sure can. In the realm of the gods, angels' helpers who form strong bonds can work together for as long as they want. Having someone tell you what to do, and who you can be with, is something that only mortal leaders and governments do."

"Tunnel Thugs," Tir translated.

All the young people around the table burst out laughing, and didn't stop for a long time.

*　*　*

Chapter 24: Epilog

Dem and Tir of Sonmatia Two, the only human brother and sister on the planet, had three days to think about the offer Feli-tala Rima had made to them.

In that time, twenty-one more couples arrived at the Angels' camp, in three separate groups. The last group reported that *everyone* had had a chance to join them, so anyone who didn't, must have been happy with mushrooms, and maybe some old canned food.

Feli-tala Rima, three other mission specialists, the regular crew of the life-monitor ship, and two others not visible to the local people, all conferred, and decided that their mission was drawing to a close.

Dem and Tir both struggled with their decision, knowing that the tunnels and caves of their childhood home, in not many years, would fall completely silent. It somehow felt right that the last people alive would be the Tunnel Thugs, eating old canned food, but having no one to sort their trash.

Finally, the tables and stools were brought into the ship. Since the refugees were all young and mal-nourished, most passenger seats easily held two. The hatch was closed by the furry steward, the feathered navigator plotted a course, and the pilot with iridescent scales guided the ship into a large pool in the back of the cavern.

With arms around each other for courage, the passengers soon beheld the sickly yellow daylight of their dead cities, then the warm white light of the Sonmatia sun, and finally the star-studded velvet of space.

Dem and Tir looked at each other, smiled, and nodded.

✳ ✳ ✳ ✳ ✳

Part 3

This part collects the stories from Sonmatia Three by winners of the past NEBADOR Writing Contests, 2010 - 2014, all of which are prequels or spin-offs of *NEBADOR Books One, Two, Three*, and *Four*. They have been placed in story-chronological order.

Rini and the Old Slave

by Terri Snyder

This story takes place about four years before Ilika arrives in the kingdom in *NEBADOR Book One: The Test*.

Rini was about nine when he wandered away from the farm where he was born for the last time. He knew his family wouldn't really miss him. He had strong brothers and sisters who were happy doing farm work. Rini didn't mind working, but he was skinny and couldn't do some of the hard work. Also, he knew there was something else out there he had to find.

The girl down the road who liked him, who was about eight, cried a little when she heard he was gone, but couldn't do anything about it. She grew up and married Rini's brother who was big and strong.

When Rini left, it was late summer and there were plenty of berries everywhere. Rini wandered into the hills near Bee, where he visited many places he liked. As he sat alone on the hills, watching the sun set over the ocean in the west, he knew this time was different. He knew he wasn't going back. He just didn't know where he was going.

For weeks he wandered in the grasslands north of the hills, playing hide and seek with the rabbits, running with the foxes, and howling with the wolves. One or two farmers heard him, but just thought it was a sick wolf.

When fall came, he walked north, thinking he could find a cave, or make a little house, in the woods. He looked through tree branches at the little village of Huk, but didn't let anyone see him. Dogs heard him and smelled him, but he was so much like a wild creature by then that they didn't even bark.

Rini found a cave, but it was taken by foxes, and they didn't want to share it. He built a little house with tree branches, but a storm knocked it down. He said thank you to the pile of tree branches and walked deeper into the woods.

The fall started getting frosty, and Rini shivered until the sun finally warmed him. He was crossing the road from Huk to Lumber Town when he found an old box that was only smashed on one side. He dragged it into the woods and made it into a house. Another storm came, but his house was strong enough this time.

✳

After a few more weeks, the days were frosty all day long, and very cold at night. Rini put dry leaves in his house, and they helped a little. Bugs sometimes tickled him when he was trying to sleep.

But he had a bigger problem. The frost made the last of the berries go moldy. He couldn't find anything to eat. Just for a moment, he thought about being a hunter. The thought made his stomach twist up into knots, so he forgot about that idea.

✳

Rini was just about to give up and get on the road to Huk, or maybe Lumber Town, to find some work he could do in trade for some food. Then he saw an old man walking very slowly in the woods. Rini hadn't talked to anyone in about two months, and he was getting a little lonely.

"Hello!" he called down from the rocks where he was sitting.

The old man shaded his old eyes and looked up. Then he walked slowly on along the path.

Rini thought the old man didn't want to talk to him, and that made him feel a little sad. But a minute later the old man came to a log and slowly lowered his old bones onto it.

"I don't know if you are a good boy, or a bad boy, but either way I could not get away from you," the old man said. "In fact, I don't think I will be going much father from here."

Rini quickly climbed down from the rocks and stood looking at the old man.

The old man looked right at Rini. "I can't see you very well, but you haven't tried to steal my pack yet, so maybe you are a good boy."

"I would never steal you pack," Rini said. "I'm just a little lonely and would like to talk to someone."

"You got anything to eat?" the old man asked.

"No," Rini said. "The berries molded, and I'm not much of a hunter."

The old man took his pack off and opened it with his stiff fingers. "Let me see. Bread to keep your belly warm, fish for your muscles, and fruit for your heart."

Rini took the pieces of food that the old man handed him, and could feel his stomach churning just smelling the food. He was about to gobble it all down, but noticed the old man eating very slowly, so Rini ate slowly too.

"What are you gonna do to survive the winter?" the old man asked after slowly eating some bread.

"I don't know," Rini said. "Maybe go to a village and ask if I can work."

The old man was silent as he ate some fish. "That might work. You'll have something to eat some days, but not others."

Rini thought about it. "What are you gonna do?" he asked.

The old man finished slowly eating a piece of dried fruit before saying anything. "There's a stream up this trail about a mile. I played there when I was little. I kissed a girl there when I was a youth. I hide there from soldiers once. It's special. I have enough food to get me there, maybe keep we warm for a week or two. That's enough."

Rini wondered how that could be enough food with winter coming, but didn't say anything.

*

Rini carried the pack as the old man slowly walk along the trail. He used his walking stick all the time, but didn't stumble much with Rini carrying the pack.

As they walked slowly along, the old man asked Rini to stay and share his food until it ran out. Rini felt guilty about eating the old man's food, and said so, but the old man told Rini it was worth it to have someone to talk to.

When the sun started to set, the old man said they were about half way there, so Rini made a little house for them with tree branches. Luckily there was no storm that night.

All the next day they walked slowly through the woods. They couldn't talk much because the old man only had enough breath for walking or talking, but not both.

Late in the day they came to the stream, and the old man almost seemed to be young again. He walked around, telling Rini about the old cabin that was falling down when he was young, and now was just a pile of rotten boards. He showed Rini the place where stones made a pool, but now some of the stones were scattered down the stream. He pointed to a piece of old rope hanging from a tree and told Rini about the swing that used to be there.

Before the sun set, Rini gathered tree branches again and made a little house for them. They ate bread and dried fish, then fell asleep.

*

The fall days after that were cold but clear. With bread in his belly, Rini stayed warm. The old man had a cloak that kept him warm. Sometimes the sun would warm them a little just before setting.

As the days passed, Rini thought about what the old man had said, and realized he wasn't going to leave his special place ever again.

*

"I was a slave most of my life," the old man said when they had been there about a week.

Rini had seen slaves, but didn't know much about it. He begged the old man to tell him more.

"Slavery happens to people who aren't smart enough to see dangers and avoid them, or smart enough to see chances and take them. That was me. Always a little too slow. I thought someone was going to hand me life on a platter. Doesn't happen that way."

"Was it a good life?" Rini asked, knowing the man was not planning to live much longer.

The old man thought for a long time. "Yes and no."

Rini looked at him and waited.

"It taught me what people are all about. I saw very good people, and very bad people. I learned to tell the difference, even before they said or did anything. And it gave me work and food every day. That was the good part of being a slave."

The old man was silent as he listened to the stream gurgling.

"What about the bad part?" Rini asked.

"The bad part was staying a slave too long. Remember what I said about being too slow to see the dangers and chances?"

Rini nodded.

"A few years as a slave, especially while you're young and strong, is good for any young man. You'd learn many things. You'd get stronger. Any softness in you would be worked off."

Rini waited because he knew the old man wasn't finished.

"But don't do what I did. Don't stay. Watch for your chances. Don't grow old as a slave. When they finally have no more use for you, you'll get some bread, fish, and fruit. Maybe an old cloak and a little pack if they like you. But winter will be coming. Winter comes every year."

✳

Three days later, their food ran out.

The old man walked around to all his favorite places again. The cabin. The pool. The swing. One place, a little grass hidden by some bushes, he never said anything about. Rini guessed that was where he kissed a girl.

The next day, the old man asked Rini to do one more thing for him. He asked Rini to move the little tree branch house up onto a low ridge that was above the stream. From there, he could see all his favorite places.

Rini knew it would be colder up there, but took the rest of the day doing what the old man asked. When he was done, he added more branches to keep out the wind.

As the sun set, the old man drank from his stream one more time, but there was nothing to eat. He asked Rini to help him up to the little house. With a far-away look in his eyes, he sat in the entrance until the light faded. Then the old man crawled inside and went to sleep.

✳

When Rini woke up the next morning, he could not wake the old man, who had become all cold and stiff.

Tears ran down Rini's cheeks. "Good bye. And thank you for everything you told me," Rini whispered.

Suddenly Rini knew why the old man had asked him to move the tree branch house. He didn't want to die by his favorite stream, and maybe ruin the water.

Rini stayed at the special place most of that day, looking at the old cabin, the pool, the broken swing, and the hidden place where a young man had once kissed a girl. Up on the ridge, he covered the entrance to the little tree branch house with more branches.

As the sun started getting low in the west, Rini walked down the trail, back the way they had come, toward the road from Huk to Lumber Town. When he came to the road, he thought for a moment, then started walking toward Huk.

*

Rini had been to Huk once before. It had a mill, a small inn, a grocer, some houses, and a little guard post. He arrived just as the sun was setting.

He looked at the inn and grocer. Both had lamps and candles lit, and people were going in and out. Rini knew both those places were for people who had copper pieces in their pouches. Rini didn't even have a pouch.

He looked at the mill. A sign said, "Need strong men." Rini glanced at his skinny arms and walked on.

Rini stood in the middle of the road remembering all the things the old man told him. He walked to the little guard post, stepped inside, and said, "I'd like to be a slave."

*   *   *

Kibi and the Search for Happiness

by Katelynn Persons

This story takes place a year and a half before Ilika arrives in the kingdom in *NEBADOR Book One: The Test*.

"Learn your place! You're a slave, our slave, and nothing more."

I stared blankly at the ground as I heard another whip lash toward me. Covering my face, I immediately yelled in pain.

"Now get moving, slave girl!" his cold voice barked as he grabbed my bruised and bleeding arms and pushed me back in line.

I watched my friends turn and look at me with knowing eyes, but not a word was spoken until the guard cracked his whip, making us yelp and whimper in fear.

"I said get moving!"

We all turned around and walked slowly back out to the field.

"Why do you let him do that, Kibi?" the tall boy asked as he looked up from his shovel.

I stared at the gashes in my arms and legs for a long time before finally looking up. "What would you do, Miko?" I asked, frustrated, careful not to let the guards hear us. "Fight back?" I jabbed my shovel back into the soft soil, throwing the dirt over my shoulder onto the pile behind us.

"I guess so . . . I don't know. Something is better then nothing."

"If you come up with a way to get out of here and not get us all killed, you let me know." I looked down at my shovel as it sliced through the rich soil again.

Miko looked slowly down at his work. "Kibi . . . I want out."

I looked up at him as he continued working slowly. "What do you mean?"

I stammered with hesitation.

"Hey!" one of the guards yelled, cracking his whip. "Get back to work!"

We nodded and quickly picked up the pace.

"I mean I want out, Kibi. There is so much more out there for me, I just know there is!"

"But, Miko," I replied, not daring to take my eyes off my shovel, "how would you ever do that? Trust me, I feel the same way you do. We're too smart to be here, we know that, they know that, everyone knows that . . . but we can't! Not right now at least. Not while those guards are looking at us."

"Kibi, I'm not stupid. I know. I'm going to get out of here, and you're not going to stop me!"

"I don't want to stop you, Miko," I quickly replied, choosing my words carefully. "I just don't want to see you get hurt!"

"I'm not going to," he replied sternly, glancing up at me. "I'm going to be free. And I'm doing it tonight. Neti will surely be on my side and go with me, even if you're too chicken."

"I don't want trouble," I replied, staring at my shovel.

"You'll never be free if there isn't any trouble, Kibi."

I stared down at the ground as I swiftly kept digging.

"I know your logic and realism are probably in the way of seeing that, but you have to put them aside and think about freedom! Isn't that what you want?"

"Of course that's what I want . . . but . . ."

Suddenly the alarm clanged and we all hit the ground, slamming our stomachs against the dirt. *Uh oh. Trouble.*

"Everyone on the ground!" one of the guards yelled.

We could see a man running through the field, one of the smaller slave boys in his arms. *It's Jalo, the young boy of about seven that I hold so dearly to my heart.*

"Jalo," I whispered softly as tears began filling my eyes and rolling down my cheeks. I knew in that moment that I might never see my little friend again.

"Another kidnapping," Miko whispered, obviously detaching himself from the situation. I didn't take my eyes off the man and crying child until they were tiny specks in the distance, some of the guards still charging after them.

"Everybody up!" the remaining guards yelled.

We all scrambled to our feet.

"Back to work!"

✳

Later that night, back in our shelter, I sat alone on my mat as a figure walked toward me. I scooted over and made room for Miko beside me.

"I'm leaving, Kibi!" his sharp words pierced my ears.

I stared ahead, emotionless. "Where do you plan on going?"

"Anywhere, anywhere but here. And Neti is going with me," he quietly but firmly responded, gesturing to the small, pretty girl sitting on a mat against a wall, holding her knees. "Are you coming?"

I looked sternly into my handsome friend's eyes. "You're serious?" I asked dryly.

"Do I look like I'm kidding? Come on, Kibi! We deserve better then this! All of us do, and you know that."

I felt my face flush as I looked at the ground for a long time.

"Are you with us or not?"

I sighed and played with a small rock, running it over my fingers and back again. "What are you planning?" I asked slowly, looking up at him.

His eyes lit up with enthusiasm. "We're going to wait until all of the guards and the master fall asleep. We'll go through the door as quietly as possible, dash through the vegetable garden, through the nook between the far cabin and the river, and out where that man took Jalo this morning."

I cringed at the memory of the little boy. "How do you plan on living? We have no money, no food, no other clothes, no shoes."

"It's better then living here," Miko responded softly. He stared at the ground for a long time. "Neti has a couple of copper pieces; she found them while digging a few weeks ago. I know a couple of others have coppers they'd be willing to give us too. That should give us enough to survive until we know what we're doing."

I looked up at him. "Why is Neti going?" I asked playfully.

He blushed a little bit. "She's one of my best friends, Kibi,"

I smirked. "You sure there isn't anything going on between you two?"

He giggled and nudged my shoulder. "She's pretty . . . and I could see myself with her, sure," he shrugged. "But . . . right now . . . I have my eye on another girl," he informed me as he looked back into my eyes.

I looked at him with slight confusion.

He leaned in and softly kissed my lips.

I kissed him back, still somewhat confused.

He gently pulled back and looked into my eyes.

I took in a deep breath; looking into his dark eyes, I told him softly, "I'm going."

✳

"Everyone is asleep," Neti whispered after she tiptoed to us in the cabin.

Miko and I looked at each other, both with unsteady stomachs.

"Guess this is it," Miko responded, swallowing.

"Now or never," I whispered back as I glanced around at my friends in the darkness for what may have been the last time.

"Are we going or not?" Neti urged. "You know they'll be up soon to keep guard. They don't think any of us knows that they leave us unguarded at this hour."

"Surely they have some sort of security system . . ." Miko started.

I grabbed his arm and looked into his unsure eyes. "Miko," I whispered. "Do you want us all to have a shot at freedom, or is your logic and realism in your way of seeing that?"

He swallowed again as he looked at me with a smirk.

"Lets go," he whispered.

We gathered our copper pieces, collected from our friends when we said our goodbyes earlier. We were sure not to mention it to anyone who would tell the guards.

Neti offered to go ahead. We let her, agreeing to follow her once she had made it.

Miko and I huddled together in the small space between two of the slave cabins, just barely wide enough for Miko's large body to fit in.

"Are you ready?" he whispered, looking into my eyes in the darkness.

"As ready as I'll ever be," I said as my stomach churned and I looked down at our feet, just inches away from each other. He took a step towards me and put his hands on my waist, pulling me to him. I looked up into his eyes as he kissed my forehead.

"We're going to make it, Kibi," he said as he ran the back of his hand down my cheek.

I smiled and put my hand over his, confused about why we went from a simple friendship, to so much more in a day. "I know . . . this has to work," I said looking into his eyes.

He smiled and kissed my lips once more. "Kibi . . . I love you."

I took a step back in confusion, looking into his eyes breathlessly. "What?" I said dumbfounded.

"I . . . I'm sorry," he stuttered. "I shouldn't have said . . ."

Suddenly we heard footsteps, and we fell to the ground in the little space, our dark clothes blending in with the rotten wood of the cabins and the dirt surrounding us.

Miko gripped my hand tightly as we both held our breath. A shadow from the moonlight came toward our niche.

Miko turned his head to silently watch. One of the slave boys about my age, fourteen going on fifteen, rounded the corner and I looked up, ready to make a dash for it.

"Zoko!" I whispered as I stood up.

"What are you guys . . ." he started.

I dashed to him and put my hand sharply over his mouth. "Shh!" I hissed into his ear. "They'll hear you!"

"We're escaping. We're getting out of here," Miko murmured quickly.

I released my grip on Zoko's mouth, as he looked at us with wide eyes.

"You guys can't leave! What about all of us? I thought you guys were kidding earlier . . ." he responded through his teeth, realization taking over.

"Well, we are leaving, Zoko. You're free to come with us. If not, go back inside," I told him sternly.

"Kibi . . . you can't go . . . we need you . . . you teach us things. And Miko . . . how are we going to do all of the work without you?"

I ran my hand down Zoko's face. "We need to go. Are you coming?" I asked softly.

"I can't go . . . I can't . . ." he said, tearing up.

I smiled weakly. "I understand. Go back inside. We'll meet again someday, I'm sure of it."

He stood there, motionless, and looked at me.

I looked back at him.

"Go on," Miko hissed, as he waved him away.

Zoko looked into my eyes and pulled me into a tight embrace.

I kissed his cheek and whispered that I'd miss him too, and to take care of himself and the young ones.

He pulled back and I saw tears glistening in the moonlight on his cheeks, just as I felt tears on my own face.

I wiped the moisture away from his eyes and he gripped my hand for a second, before he quickly turned and went back inside his cabin.

Miko put his hand on my shoulder as I fought back a waterfall of tears. He tenderly wrapped his arms around my shoulders and held me against his warm chest, where I cried. I cried for the unknown, I cried for little Jalo, I cried for the friends I was leaving behind, I cried for my confusion about Miko, and I cried for my future.

✳

We met Neti in the garden behind a tool shed. Neti embraced us both when she saw we had made it okay.

"We need to hurry," Neti declared. "Dawn is coming soon. They will catch us easier if that happens."

Miko and I nodded. "Run quickly, and quietly until we reach the nook where the cabin meets with the line of the river. We'll cross there," I said quickly, looking at them both.

Miko and Neti nodded as they glanced at each other.

"I'll take the lead," I continued. "Follow me once I make it behind the cabin. Follow quickly, and one at a time. But we don't have too much time."

They both nodded with understanding and I peeked out from behind the tool shed. Everything was still, and hadn't moved. So with one look back at Miko and Neti, more specifically Miko, I took in a deep breath and walked low and quickly through the tall wheat and grass. After dodging a couple of holes that had been dug into the ground earlier that day, I found myself behind the cabin. I breathed deeply as I waited for the next person to come running. I leaned back against the cabin wall and looked up as I closed my eyes, trying to catch my breath and settle the butterflies in the pit of my stomach. *Am I really doing this?*

Next thing I knew, Neti came around the corner, out of breath. She smiled and threw her arms around me for a long embrace.

"How are you holding up?" I supportively responded, rubbing her back.

She nodded into my neck and shoulder.

I pulled back and smiled.

"Miko will be here soon," she whispered, her face getting a little pale, even through the darkness.

"What's wrong, Neti?" I asked with uncertainty. She looked down, but said nothing. "Neti?"

"Kibi," she said finally. "How ... how do you feel about Miko?" She looked timidly into my eyes.

I took in a breath and rested my hands on my waist. "Honestly, Neti?" I admitted, letting out a breath. "I don't know right now. Why do you ask?"

She ran her tattered shoe through the dirt and back again. "I think he likes you."

I hesitated. "I think so too," I said, nodding as I tripped over my thoughts. "But at the same time, I think he's just confused, with everything that's going on. I think he's taking his emotions for me as a friend to unprincipled extents. Why do you bring it up?"

She looked down for a long time, and then back into my eyes. "Kibi ... I think I love Miko."

✳

"Made it!" Miko said rounding the corner.

Neti smiled and wiped away the tears that our conversation had brought to her eyes.

Miko immediately wrapped me in his arms to embrace me. I smiled weakly and accepted a short hug. I kept urging Neti with my eyes to embrace him next, which she did with grace, as she does everything else. I couldn't help but feel a hint of jealousy as she held him ... jealousy that she wanted him too.

"Now what?" Neti said, reluctantly leaving Miko's grip.

I forced myself to smile, before bringing my focus back to the task at hand. "The bridge over the stream is down there," I said, pointing to the left of us about fifty feet. "But it's through an open field. So we'll have to move quickly and not look back. Neti, I'd like you to go first this time. Once you get across, I want you to go a little ways into the forest, and hide behind the first large tree you find. When Miko and I come across, one at a time, we'll whisper your name. I want you to whisper your name when you hear us coming to you, and we'll hide beside you until all three of us are across. Got it?"

Neti nodded with a gleam of eagerness surrounding her face. "Keep watch for me, just in case anyone's coming," she whispered uncertainly.

I smiled. "Of course, Neti. Now go, we all need to get across."

She nodded solemnly as she scanned the area around her before quickly making her way down to the bridge.

We watched her for a moment before I lost sight of her in the darkness and leaned back against the wall. I remembered Miko's presence beside me and smirked, happy to be alone with him again. I looked up at him and smiled once our eyes met.

He came closer and slid his arm around my waist, gently kissing my neck and whispering in my ear how much he cared about me.

I smiled as a chill went down my spine, and wrapped my arms around him. He held me against his chest for a long time, before finally kissing my lips and letting me go.

"I better get moving," I murmured reluctantly. "We have a lot of ground to cover."

"Of course," he said, running his fingertips down my cheek.

I smiled as the butterflies flooded my stomach once again, and observed my surroundings as I made my way across the open field and across the rickety bridge, taking a last look back at Miko's figure in the darkness. I looked ahead of me and ran forward, whispering Neti's name over and over until I heard a faint whisper coming from behind one of the trees. I stopped and listened to where it came from. I whispered her name again and she stepped out from behind a large oak tree. I jumped before I realized it was her.

"Shh, Kibi! It's only me!" she said as she took a step towards me.

I put my hand over my quickening heart as I went and hid behind the large tree with her, neither of us saying much of anything until Miko showed up, where we both unconsciously and jealously fought for his affection.

We soon were walking through the large, dark forest, all of us making small talk. Miko held my hand for a while, which I felt fortunate for. I really did care for Miko . . . and still I felt guilty about Neti. She had been trying so hard to get him to notice her. We kept walking through the forest until dawn rose. I looked at Neti as she yawned.

"We should probably get some rest," I said finally.

Miko looked at me and I saw Neti smile briefly at the idea.

"Here look good?" Miko suggested as we came into a clearing with trees, and minimal rocks covering the ground.

Neti and I nodded and immediately found trees to sleep against for the night. I sat against a large tree and leaned my back against it, closing my eyes.

Neti was soon fast asleep, with her girly little snore that made me giggle to myself.

Suddenly I heard slow footsteps and my eyes shot open. It was Miko coming to sit next to me. As I had done earlier that evening, I scooted over to the side and Miko sat down with me. Soon Miko has his arms around my waist and I was nuzzled into his chest, fast asleep.

✳

"No! Neti!" I heard a voice yell as my eyes flashed open, squinting instantly at the bright morning sun.

Men were surrounding us and had Neti's arms held back, one man throwing her over his shoulder.

"Neti!" I screamed, scrambling to my feet. I ran and hit the man who was holding her, obviously not fazing him any as he grunted and shoved me to the ground, yelling at another man in a foreign tongue and pointing to me.

I felt Miko jump over me to protect me, just to get thrown down by a large man with a whip.

The man holding Neti started to run and I grabbed his ankle. As I made him stumble, he let go of Neti, who instantly fell to the ground. I saw Miko run to her aid, and hold her to his chest as she yelled about a pain in her arm.

A small man picked me up and swung me over his shoulder as I kicked and screamed. I saw Miko grab Neti's waist, and even through my conscious jealousy, I yelled for them to run.

Neti held Miko's hand as she went to take off into the forest. Miko reluctantly followed behind her, staring back at me with regretful eyes.

I nodded and mouthed for them to go, and saw a tear falling down his cheek as he turned to run with Neti back into the forest.

*

"You really thought you'd get away, didn't you, girl?" the man holding me asked with amusement.

"It's Kibi," I responded bitterly.

He and the two men following just laughed.

The large man that had thrown Miko to the ground was following us, and ran his hand down my cheek. "Pretty girl. What business do you have in the forest?"

I coldly pulled my face back. "Independence, just out of my grasp. If you lugs wouldn't have held me back, I may possibly have had it by now!"

The man smacked me across the face as I yelped. "You will talk to us like superiors. Words like that should not be said from the tongue of someone like you. Shut up before I shut you up."

Tears filled my eyes in pain as I felt a trickle of blood slide down my cheek from where he had struck me, but I remained strong and held back my tears.

"Your friends may have escaped us this far, but they'll be back," the third man informed me with a chuckle.

I stared back the way we came, soberly wondering where my friends were now.

*

"Kibi!" all of my friends yelled as I entered the cabin. Hugs and kisses surrounded me instantly.

Tears filled my eyes once again at the sight of my brothers, sisters, friends, and what I considered to be my family.

"You came back," I heard a boy's voice say as I looked through everyone surrounding me. It was Zoko.

I smirked with a hint of embarrassment as he smiled. I broke through the crowd and went to him.

"I hoped that you'd make it," he uttered softly as he looked into my eyes.

I smiled. "Yeah, I wish we all would have," I murmured with sadness in my voice, staring down at the insecure floorboards of the leaky cabin. I felt Zoko hold me in a warm embrace, which felt good after so much uncertainty. His friendship comforted me, even if only for that brief moment.

"Where are the others?" he asked me through our teary-eyed hug.

A tear fell down my cheek as I whispered that I didn't know.

He held me tighter. "Maybe they made it," he said, trying to reassure himself, more then me, of his confidence.

"Thanks," I said, running my hand up and down his back before reluctantly pulling away from his arms.

He smiled and ran his hand down my arm.

"Okay excitement over! Everyone get to work!" the guards said as they threw shovels, plows and gloves outside of our cabins.

We impulsively jumped as we all headed outside.

I ran and grabbed my routine shovel and gloves, when I felt a hand on my shoulder.

"Oh no no no, pretty miss. We have a special day planned for you." I took a deep breath and turned around: the guard who had smacked me.

※

I kept my eyes closed the entire time; whip after whip after whip, screaming as I felt my blood trickling down my body, wearing only my torn and tattered rags for protection.

"Get in there!" I heard a voice yell as the beating came to a pause.

I saw two guards come in, and throw Miko and Neti onto the ground beside me.

"Miko! Neti!" I yelled, instantly grabbing them both in a hug and kissing Miko's cheek, all of us crying.

"Get off!" the cruel man yelled as he whipped us all.

We screamed and jumped back, each of us getting whipped by separate masters.

They beat us and beat us and beat us, until they finally wore me down and I couldn't fight back. I fell down onto the brick floor, holding my body, my head hidden by my arms as he whipped me mercilessly.

※

I opened my eyes hesitantly, only to reveal a layer of darkness surrounding me. I went to sit up slowly, but instantly shot back down. I looked around, only daring to move my neck at this point. It was a dark room with one small window up in the corner, letting in a stream of pale moonlight. I looked across the room to see Neti and Miko fast asleep, holding each other. As much as it pained me to see them that way, so happy together, I kept my focus on the throbbing pain in my ribs. I had obviously cracked one of them when I hit the brick floor after being beaten. I looked around the room; it was one of the security cabins for any wannabe runaways, which was now being kept guarded during all hours.

I looked back over at Miko and Neti, and saw Miko looking back at me.

I smiled weakly as tears filled my eyes.

He gently untangled his arms from around my pretty friend, and came to sit beside me. He touched my shoulder gently and looked into my eyes.

"She loves you," I muttered weakly, holding back tears.

He nodded solemnly. "I know, Kibi."

I looked down at my shattered ribcage, trying to imagine myself anywhere but there. "Do you love her?" I asked, not daring to look at him in fear of me completely losing it.

"Yes, Kibi," he sighed, "I love her."

I closed my eyes in pain, both emotional and physical, as tears ran slowly down my cheeks. I felt his hand being removed from my shoulder. "I am so sorry." He whispered softly, as he went to stand up.

I held his arm to keep him there. "It's ... okay, Miko," I said dryly, surprised that I could say it honestly. "You two have always been cute together."

He smiled. "Thanks, Kibi ... that really means a lot ... coming from you."

I smiled weakly as he kissed my cheek, stood up and went to a mat in the far corner of the cabin by himself, curling up and going to sleep.

Tomorrow is another day, I thought to myself. I lay there and remembered my tender moments with Miko, and the not so pleasant past; the fighting, the anger, and the most recent affairs with one another. How could I have thought it would ever last? His heart is obviously with Neti. But, as long as Miko's happy, I guess I'm happy too. I closed my eyes as I felt a cool breeze coming in through the high-up window. I put my hands gently on my cracked ribcage for comfort, and softly drifted off to sleep to the sound of my friend's breathing.

✳

"Kibi," he said looking up into the stars. "What do you see?"

I smiled and ran my hands down his arms. "A beautiful starry night."

"What are those stars, Kibi?" he said looking at me tenderly.

I looked back at him, smiling, then back at the stars up above. "Holes in the sky. The universe shedding little lights."

The man laughed and kissed my forehead. "My Kibi," he whispered softly.

I nuzzled into his shoulder and looked up into his eyes.

He looked down at me and kissed my lips.

I gazed into his eyes, and felt a wave of comfort come over me, being completely at peace with life. Something that I had never known existed until lying there, in that man's arms. "Thank you," I whispered through my tears, "so much."

The man smiled and pulled me close to him. "Go to sleep, Kibi. You deserve it."

I rested my head on his chest and gently closed my eyes, thinking that maybe this world wasn't such a bad place after all.

I felt him kiss my forehead and whisper words of affection in my ear, as I fell into a deep sleep.

✳

I woke up to the bright sunlight streaming in through the window high above me.

I looked around and saw Miko and Neti gone, but I was covered in the old blanket that Neti was using last night, and felt the comfort of my friends.

I lay there, and recalled my dreams of that night. I dreamt of a man, a slightly older man, one I had fallen for. I couldn't recall the young man's name, but he was smart, very smart. He taught me words that I didn't even know existed, even with my large vocabulary. I couldn't recall if he was another slave boy ... but he seemed too educated and well dressed to be a slave, and I couldn't imagine him being a slave master or guard. We didn't look like we were in a slave camp ... and I don't remember ever seeing his face in real life. All I knew for sure was that there was something about that dream that called to me. Maybe Miko isn't the one for me ... he's Neti's man. I'll just have to find my own dream man some day. The one that will hold me like Miko holds Neti, and kiss me how Miko kissed me, except actually mean it. I smiled softly as I took one last look around, and snuggled into the comfort of my blanket, drifting back into sleep, into my dream man's world for one last visit.

✳   ✳   ✳

First Taste of Freedom

By Katelynn Persons

This story takes place when Miko and Neti are buying pouches in the marketplace and the nearby streets of Rumble Town in *NEBADOR Book One: The Test.*

Miko and Neti stepped into Rumble Town for the first time on their own, with nothing but each other and the money pouch Ilika had given them with two small silver and eight copper pieces inside.

"Where do we go?" handsome Miko asked uncertainly as he stared uneasily into the busy streets of Rumble Town.

Neti looked around, more determined than frightened. "Well," she said, thinking, "Ilika said we need to do some of the shopping for the group. We need money pouches, enough for all eight of us, so we need to find somewhere that sells them, preferably somewhere close."

Miko looked at Neti with shifting eyes. "What if we get lost?"

"We won't," the pretty girl said as she took her love's hand. "Trust me."

He nodded as he looked timidly down the street, and followed Neti's lead into the crowd, in hopes of completing their first task.

✳

"Look!" Neti exclaimed as she pointed to a group of large, rich-looking men on horses coming toward them.

Miko watched the men approach as his stomach tightened. "Our old slave masters," he whispered under his breath.

They stood frozen for a few moments of panic before Neti took Miko's hand and led him into the crowd, going away from the terrible men. Miko stopped in his tracks.

"No, Neti!" he said firmly.

She turned around, almost running into him. "What are you doing?" she asked with a hiss.

Miko took her hands in his as he looked into her startled eyes. "Neti, we aren't slaves anymore, there's nothing to be afraid of! Ilika said to treat everyone we come across with respect, so we can't run from them. We have to continue what we're doing, or they'll think we're acting suspiciously."

Neti looked at him anxiously, but gave him a small nod of understanding.

He smiled and touched her cheek gently. "Come on, there's a leather wagon over there, maybe they'll have what we need."

Without a word of disagreement, Neti followed Miko to a small wagon filled with different leather goods. Miko reached down to make sure the coin pouch was still on his belt as he and Neti looked around the wagon with eager eyes.

"There!" Neti said with excitement as she rushed to the other end of the cart, picking up a brown coin pouch off the wagon. "How much for this?" she asked the leather man as Miko scurried to her side.

The leather man turned to face the pretty girl, and saw the nervous boy standing beside her. With a pause for thought, he responded, "One copper piece and it's yours."

Neti smiled at Miko as he untied his pouch and dug out a copper piece, handing it to the man.

"Thank you very much!" he called back at the man as he followed Neti into the crowd.

⁕

"Those sweet biscuits smell so good!" Miko said as they ambled past the baked-goods cart.

"I know," Neti said slowly, "but Ilika might be mad if we spend his money on treats. We have to find money pouches for the rest of us."

"You're right," Miko said slowly with disappointment.

"One copper for three biscuits!" the man said to Neti and Miko as they passed.

"Really?" Miko said, then received a disapproving glance from Neti. "I mean, no thank you."

Neti smiled and took his hand again, leading him past the lingering aroma of sweets.

They passed one of the bread carts, stocked with good-smelling breads and rolls, but with their stomachs still full from breakfast, it wasn't as hard to pass them up as the sweets had been.

"Hey, Neti," Miko began as they continued walking, "what do you think of Ilika so far?"

"Ilika?" she responded, her eyes examining the ground in front of her. "He's alright, I guess. I don't really understand the point of all this, though."

"Me neither," Miko said, shaking his head, "I was just curious. He seems so different from the rest of us. I don't get why he's treating us this way. For all he knows, we could be escaping right now."

"I know, it's weird, but I'm not going to complain. He bought us our freedom. He said that we could leave whenever we wanted and he wouldn't try to stop us."

"But he trusts us with his money. Why would he do that if we're free to walk away?" Miko asked, noticing Neti's thoughtful expression as she pondered the question.

"I don't know. He's just a very trusting person, I guess. I just hope he's not so blind that he trusts Kodi with his money."

"Or anything, for that matter," Miko said with a smile.

Neti smiled back and kissed her man.

"Alright," she said, looking around, "where would we find more money pouches? I don't remember."

Miko looked around. "What about that little shop over there?" Miko said as he looked at Neti for approval before heading that way.

Inside, they found exactly what they needed, money pouches of all different colors and designs.

"These are perfect!" Neti said with excitement, picking one up. "The different colors will make it easy to tell them apart if they get mixed up!"

"Right!" Miko said as he chose two colors. "How many more do we need?"

Neti thought for a moment. "Well, if we need eight, and we have one . . . that's eight minus one."

Miko put down the pouches and subtracted slowly on his fingers. "Seven pouches!" he stated as he picked up a few more. When they had all they needed, they joyfully approached the shopkeeper.

"We'd like to buy these, please," Neti said in her most polite voice, setting the seven pouches in front of the shopkeeper.

"Alright," said the large man slowly, "that'll be seven coppers."

Neti looked eagerly at Miko as he slowly counted out his coppers from the money pouch.

"Seven coppers," Miko said, handing them to the shopkeeper.

"Thank ya kindly," said the man. "Have a good day now!"

Neti and Miko smiled as they carried their new merchandise away from the counter. Suddenly they heard the large old man holler at them. "Hey you kids! Get back here with them money pouches!"

They stopped in their tracks. Their skin became cold and pale as they turned to face the man, who approached them and took the pouches from their hands.

"Trying to steal one of my pouches?" the man quickly accused. "Do you know what the penalty is for stealing?"

"We . . . we didn't steal anything," Neti said, trying to keep her voice from shaking.

"You've already been caught, stop lying!" the man said as he went back to the counter and set the pouches in a row. "You see these right here? You bought seven pouches from me, yes?"

"That's right . . ." Miko replied cautiously.

"Then would you mind counting how many of them are lying on this counter?"

Neti, lacking good counting skills, turned to Miko in fright, who slowly approached the counter. He counted out loud, one by one.

"There are eight pouches here," Miko said softly, "but we had already bought one from another place."

"You expect me to believe that crud? Get out of here, and don't you two dare come back!"

"No, honestly!" Neti said, fighting back tears. "We would never steal from you! Please believe us . . ."

"Prove your innocence!" the man said firmly.

Neti, with determination written on her face, approached the counter and picked up the money pouch from the cart. "See this one? It's different from all of these you sell. The ones we bought from you have different colors and patterns, so there's no way we could have stolen this one if you don't sell them!"

The man examined the pouches with careful eyes before looking back at Neti, trying to hide her trembling. He sighed and handed the pouches back to them. "My apologies," he said in a deep, rough voice. "Be careful, and don't bring things like that into other stores or you'll get yourself in some *real* trouble, do you hear me?"

"Yes, sir," Neti and Miko said at once as they picked up the pouches and hurried out of the shop.

They stopped and sat on a street corner, setting the pouches next to them. Neti broke into tears.

"Oh, Neti," Miko said, wrapping his arms around the pretty girl, "there's no reason to cry, we didn't do anything wrong!"

"I know," Neti said between sobs, "but we could have let Ilika down! What if the shopkeeper didn't believe us?"

"Shh," Miko coaxed, "no reason to talk like that. Your quick thinking got us out of there, and that's what counts." He wiped the tears quietly from her face as she calmed down. Then he kissed her forehead before saying, "Let's get back to Ilika before he thinks something's wrong."

Neti nodded and thanked him softly, but Miko only smiled and took her hand as they stood up, each of them carrying a few of the pouches.

✳

Neti and Miko walked side by side the entire way back to the inn, making small talk about their friends, and about Ilika.

"This life is a lot better than the one we had, that's for sure," Miko said with a soft smile.

"Yeah . . . it's sure different."

Miko smirked as he thoughtfully said, "Remember that time where you, me, and Kibi honestly thought we could escape?"

"Yeah," Neti said dryly. "I do."

"Doesn't seem so crazy now!" Miko declared.

Neti looked down and shuffled her feet, something she hadn't done before.

"I hit a nerve . . ." Miko began softly. "What is it?"

Neti shook her head quickly. "It's nothing, just remembering."

"Remembering what?" Miko questioned with raised eyebrows.

Neti stopped and put her hand on Miko's shoulder.

He turned around to face his girl. Seeing her seriousness, he whispered, "What is it?"

"Miko," Neti said softly, "do . . . do you still have feelings for her?"

The handsome boy's face flushed, as he immediately knew she was speaking of Kibi.

Neti looked at him anxiously. "Well?"

"No . . . no, Neti . . . not at all." He wrapped his arms around her. "It's just me and you, I promise. I care about her, but she's a close friend, nothing more. She will never be anything more, no matter what."

"Tell me this much," Neti said, fighting back tears, "tell me that you've never actually loved her."

"I swear to you, Neti," Miko said softly.

Neti gently wiped the tears from her face.

Miko leaned in to kiss her. "You're my girl, Neti, and you always will be. No need to worry about silly things like that, alright?" he said tenderly.

"Alright."

Miko kissed her again. "Let's head back, and let other people have a chance to go out, okay?"

"Okay," Neti said as she took her man's arm, and wandered back through the streets of Rumble Town, not knowing when she'd get another moment alone with Miko.

✳   ✳   ✳

Buna's New World

By Karen Buchanan

This story takes place when Buna and Toli are buying sweets in the marketplace in *NEBADOR Book One: The Test*.

Buna danced into the marketplace.
"What are you doing?" Toli asked. "Everyone's gonna stare at us!"
"So what! There's nothing wrong with dancing."
"But Ilika said to watch out for each other, and so I'm watching out for you."
Buna stopped prancing and thought about it. "I guess you're right. I'm just . . . really happy! I haven't been able to just walk around since . . . I don't know . . . since I was a little kid. It feels *wonderful!*"
"We're supposed to buy something for dessert."
"Hmm . . ." Buna started to say, looking around. "There's tarts at the bakery . . ."
Toli scanned the marketplace, looking over most people's heads. "I think we should look at everything, then decide. Everything sweet, I mean."
Buna pouted for a moment, then grinned and nodded.

*

After whispering to the tall boy and the tangle-haired girl, the sweet biscuits thought about standing up on the table and dancing, but the woman who made them was watching, so they didn't.
Candies winked and wiggled, especially when the candy maker had his back turned. The girl holding hands with the tall boy caught a glimpse of them, but when she got close, the man was looking, so they stayed still.
A big bowl of plums, from a farm in the southern valley where hot water gushed out of the ground, could feel the girl's feet moving to the music. They

wanted so much to jump up and dance, and then send plums home with her and the tall boy. They started to wiggle, but the farmer turned around after selling carrots to the innkeeper's son, so they stopped moving and tried to look like a plain, innocent bowl of plums.

✳

As they walked among the carts, Buna leaned on Toli and looked up at him. "What do you think of this weird master we have?"

"He's not a master, he's a captain."

"Oh, yeah. What's it like working on a ship?"

"About like being a slave, I think. I've unloaded ships, but not sailed on them. I think you have to be good with ropes and stuff to be a sailor."

Buna frowned. "But you can leave, right?"

Toli laughed. "Only at a port!"

Buna thought about it, then snickered.

✳

A donkey eating hay saw the girl prance by, her feet still tapping to the music as she walked. The donkey listened, and heard the drum rhythm that was the same as what the girl's feet were doing.

The shaggy brown animal felt something special, like it had just seen a spirit. It knew about wolf spirits and mountain lion spirits, and how dangerous they were. But this girl seemed like a different kind of spirit, a nice spirit.

In a burst of courage, like it had never felt before, the donkey decided to try it. Front hooves started lifting up from the ground, one at a time. Once in a while, they tapped against each other.

Feeling its heart beat faster with the thrill of doing something a spirit could do, back hooves started lifting, then tapping.

Suddenly a booted foot jabbed the brown donkey in the ribs, it stumbled sideways over some wooden crates, and landed on its side, calling loudly in pain and confusion.

"Stupid donkey!" the man said, almost spitting out the words.

The donkey stayed on its side until the man left, then slowly got back to its feet.

It always remembered the girl-spirit, now long gone, but never again tried to dance.

✳

Buna and Toli sat down on a log to think about what they had seen.

"I think we should get plums!" she said excitedly.

"They looked good, but I don't think they were ripe."

Buna frowned. "Okay, sweet biscuits!"

"There were only six left. We need ten of something."

Buna sighed.

"*I've* never had a sweet biscuit . . ." a timid voice said.

Buna and Toli both looked. On the other end of the log, a little girl sat holding a bundle of cloth in her arms, and looking at them with big brown eyes.

Buna hopped up. "Maybe *we* can't decide, but *you* are getting a sweet biscuit, little friend!"

"But we're not supposed to . . ." Toli started to say, but Buna was gone.

A minute later she returned, sat down beside the little girl, and handed her the sweet biscuit. "Now there are only *five*," Buna said, looked at Toli, and stuck out her tongue.

Soon a poor woman came by and the little girl hopped up.

"Mommy, she gave me a sweet biscuit!"

The woman looked at Buna with eyes that said *thank you*. She looked in her bag for something to give in return, but found only a crust of bread.

Buna shook her head, fished in her pouch, and handed a silver piece to the woman. It brought a smile that was missing several teeth.

When the girl and her mother were gone, Toli stood beside Buna. "I'm sorry I snapped at you."

Buna looked up at the tall, handsome boy, and kissed him on the cheek. "I think the baker probably still has plenty of pastries."

"Let's go see!"

✳

Three crows perched on the inn roof.

"I could have snatched that sweet biscuit, right out of the little brat's hand, if her *mommy* hadn't shown up!" said Ke.

Te cackled. "Afraid of an old hag? That's not like you, Ke! Did you see the crust of bread she had?"

"What I see, I eat!" said Re.

"In your dreams!" Ke taunted. "Let's see what the tangle-haired girl and the tall boy get. They're heading for the bakery."

"You do recon, Ke. As soon as we know what's on the menu, I'll create a diversion, then Te swoops in for the first grab. Ke and me will be right behind for clean-up."

The three cawed at once.

✳

A slave boy, about nine years old, was cleaning up the marketplace that evening after all the wagons and carts had left. He liked working in the evening because he could look up and see the stars come out.

He didn't dare look up for very long, of course, or a whip would make him get back to work. But he knew how to take a quick look, memorize what he saw, then cherish it in his mind until he could glance up again.

As he was picking up some scraps of rope and broken pottery near a log, he happened to spot a small piece of a sweet biscuit down in the dirt, partly hidden by the log. He quickly picked it up but just held it in his hand with two fingers and continued to work.

A guard glanced at him but didn't see anything wrong.

The boy waited until he tossed the junk into the trash wagon, then as he turned to go back to work, popped the little piece of sweet biscuit into his mouth.

Even with a little dirt, it tasted heavenly.

As soon as he could, he glanced up at the darkening sky to see what stars were out. Only the brightest ones were shining.

He smiled to himself and wondered if maybe he could somehow visit them someday. Maybe he could find a way if he got free and climbed the highest mountain.

As he started picking up horse droppings, he wondered if they had sweet biscuits in the stars.

*

It was nearly midnight before Te came out from under the little cart where he had been struggling with his painful broken wing for hours. He hadn't seen the baker's broom handle coming, but clearly remembered the guard's sword slice through Re's body, then seconds later Ke fell from the sky, pierced by a feathered shaft.

Te looked around, and wondered how he was going to find somewhere safe before a dog or cat found him.

* * *

Sata's Strength

by Chenice Louise Clarke

Sata reflects on her life and values upon walking into the large bay in *NEBADOR Book Two: Journey*.

I remember when I would wipe tables and run errands for mother and father at the inn. I would be so happy if a guest would give me a coin, just one small coin, and I remember thinking I was the luckiest girl in the world — well maybe not the world, but in the capital city at least. I would work hard every day to show my father that I was just as strong and able as my brother, even though I knew that no matter how hard I tried, my brother would still be given the inn. That's how it had been in the past, and my father wasn't about to change any rules like that any time soon.

When Ilika came to stay at our inn, of all the places he could have gone, I knew that I had a chance — maybe only a tiny chance, but still a chance — that I could do something like have an adventure and learn new things.

I was so scared when I asked Ilika if he would consider girls on his trip, and I remember I nearly dropped the plate I was holding, but was very happy with his answer. I think maybe he was shocked I asked him that question, but I had to ask — I don't know any girls that are allowed to do the same things as boys, and that's not fair! I do miss the inn a lot, but looking at the bay now with my teacher and friends, I know that I made the right choice to leave, and I'm happy mother and father allowed me to go.

I remember during one of Ilika's lessons, asking him what I should do if two people asked me for something at the same time. I thought I would have to answer them both really quickly and not give a full answer so that I didn't upset either person. It reminded me when mother would ask me to fetch some spices and father would ask me to wash the floor. I would worry that one of them may be upset with me, so I tried to do both at the same time, which was very hard and often impossible. I wish I had realized then that sometimes you just have to choose the most important question first and answer it. Sometimes it's hard but I now know that even if another person is a little upset with me, once I explain why I answered someone else first, they will understand why I made that decision.

That's what I like about my new family — we talk a lot. We talk about our feelings and our decisions and our hopes, and that never happened back at the inn. My brother would ignore me, and my parents were always busy helping the guests at the inn. I guess back home I always respected my parents, but I also feared them in the same way I feared the steam vent — like I told Ilika when we were talking about the area in general. I was scared and Ilika told me that while I should respect and be careful of the steam vent, I should never fear it. I didn't know that before.

It was tough being at the steam vent, but I know that I had to stay that extra day to make peace with the land and myself so I could move on. I didn't want to be scared of another steam vent, should I see one again, or anything else I had never seen before. It's kind of like leaving the inn and my family — it was scary because I didn't know what was going to happen. I didn't know if Ilika would decide he had made a wrong decision, even though I tried and still try to be a really good student. I answer questions and make sure I do my share, like back home, so that's why I arranged for the pouches of salt, dried sage, and dried onions back at the farmer's cottage. I wanted to show my new family that I would be a good crew member because not only was working at the inn kind of like a crew, but I'm starting to think life is full of lots of little crews.

I get scared because even though I try really hard, I feel like sometimes there are other people who are better than me. That feeling upsets me because I want to do well and be chosen for Ilika's crew. I want to see if Ilika's ship has white sails because I like the color white. White is clean and it reminds me of when mother and I would put clean sheets on the guests' beds at the inn. It's like a new start and I like that. I like that you can make a new start, and even though I'm only 10, a new start is always a good idea ... sometimes. I think that Ilika gave me a new start when he came into the inn and he decided that I could come on this journey with him. Despite being scared of the stream vent, thinking I was going to die, I didn't. I think that I'm going to be okay now. Actually, I know I'm going to be okay. I'm going to be okay because I want to be okay, and if I want something enough and work for it enough, I can do it. I think that means I can be part of Ilika's crew.

I look at Boro and Mati, and all of my other new friends, and I see that even though they were slaves and dealt with terrible things, they all have hope and they're all strong. I think that one day I can be strong like them. Sure, I have strong arms from my hard work at the inn, but I want to be strong in my mind. I think I'm getting stronger every day. I mean I don't get scared so quickly now. Also, I trust more and I think that's important to being happy and being on Ilika's crew. Actually, trusting is very important which is why I trusted Ilika. More than that, that's why I trusted myself. That's why I still trust myself.

* * *

Neti's Temptation

By Karen Buchanan

This story takes place the morning after the group is trapped by high tide on the rocky coast in *NEBADOR Book Two: Journey.*

Neti couldn't sleep. She didn't toss and turn because she didn't want to wake Miko, so she just looked up at the sky and counted stars. It was kind of fun because she had just learned to count not long before.

But soon she got bored with it. Something that happened the day before really bothered her. For the first time in months, maybe years, she wasn't sure if Miko was the right boy for her.

After lying there for a long time, sometimes counting stars and sometimes just fuming, she saw a little morning light creep into the sky. She carefully slipped out from under her blankets.

"Neti?" Miko called in a groggy voice.

"Have to pee," she whispered.

"Ok, good ni . . ."

Neti tiptoed through the camp, being careful not to wake anyone. Ilika and Kibi were snuggled close, and Buna and Toli were near each other but not touching. Boro and Sata weren't sleeping close together yet, but Neti knew they would be someday. When she got near the beach, she climbed a small sand dune partly covered with wiry grass. She sat down on top and looked out over the wide beach and the calm water of the bay.

With her chin in her hands, she sat with her feelings, but no clear thoughts about anything came to her. Suddenly a sea gull landed on a nearby driftwood log and looked up at her.

"What is it about boys?" she asked the sea gull.

The sea gull cocked it head but didn't say anything.

"I suppose you might be a boy. If you are, maybe you know the answer. Why do we love boys, but they're never as good as we think they should be?"

The sea gull squawked at Neti.

She felt in her cloak pocket and found a little piece of stale bread. "You're lucky. There was a time this would have been my breakfast, and I wouldn't have shared it with you! Here you go!" She tossed the bread toward the driftwood log.

The sea gull kept an eye on Neti as it hopped off the log and grabbed the bread. Before it got back to its log, a man came walking along the beach, so the bird spread its wing and took off.

"Hey! You didn't answer my question!"

But the sea gull didn't come back, so Neti gave up and looked at the man. She knew she should go back to the camp and wake someone, just in case the man gave her any trouble, but she was still in a bad mood because of Miko, so she stayed on top of the dune.

The man wasn't very old, maybe about Ilika's age, and was dressed like any fisherman. He carried a bucket brimming with clams. When he got close, he stopped and looked up at Neti.

"Hello, fair maiden."

Neti could feel her heart pounding. "Hello."

"Are you all alone?"

"Sort of."

He came closer, and Neti could see that he was handsome. Her heart pounded louder.

"Would you like to help me clean these clams, then make a stew? My house is not far."

Neti couldn't speak for a minute, so she coughed and tried to breathe. The young man noticed her confusion and smiled.

"Um . . . maybe . . . if you'll answer a question for me first."

"If it will help me win your heart, I'll tell you anything!"

That's what Neti was afraid of. Maybe the sea gull hadn't been so bad. But she took a breath and decided to give it a try. "Why do girls always think boys are so wonderful and perfect, but they never are?"

The young fisherman squirmed and shrugged. "Um . . . because . . . no . . . maybe because . . . I don't know . . ."

Now Neti was *sure* the sea gull had been more honest.

Suddenly the young man found his thoughts and said, "I guess girls are just made that way, and boys . . . are made like they are!"

Neti thought about his answer, then asked, "So what would you do if you were in a waterfall bowl and the tide was rising?"

"Easy. Sing fishing songs until the tide went out, or carve a piece of driftwood if I had my knife."

"And if you came to a place where there's hot steam hissing out of the ground?"

He backed up, frowned, and made signs to protect himself from evil.

"That's from the Underworld, and I wouldn't go near the place without a priest at my side!"

Neti smiled. She had just learned something, but knew she couldn't tell the young, handsome fisherman. She almost wished the sea gull would come back.

The fisherman, with his bucket of clams, was still frowning. "Did you go near such a place? Places like that can put curses on people, you know."

Neti laughed out loud.

"Mocking spirits and demons is dangerous!" He looked around with fear in his eyes. "Are you going to clean these clams with me, or not? If you won't, there's a girl up the beach about a mile who will."

Neti was torn, just for a moment. Then she smiled and said, "I'm glad you have someone to share your clams with. I think . . . I'll stay here."

"Good day to you," he said with a slight bow and headed along the beach, swinging his bucket of clams and whistling.

Neti stayed on the sand dune for another half hour, thinking about what she had learned. The sea gull came back, and another, and they walked back and forth on the driftwood log, sometimes looking at each other, sometimes clicking their beaks together. Neti somehow knew that one of them was a boy, the other a girl, but she couldn't tell which was which. She decided not to interrupt them with her thoughts, so she just watched.

After a few minutes, both sea gulls looked at Neti and squawked, but she didn't have any more bread, so they flew away together.

When she finally tiptoed back to camp, Miko was still dead asleep, but Ilika was just coming out of the trees, so she went up to him, smiling.

"Guess what I just learned!" she said.

✳   ✳   ✳

What're Friends For?

by Katelynn Persons

This story takes place in *NEBADOR Book Two: Journey*, just after Boro gets a marriage proposal from Josa, and Ilika tries to reassure Sata that it will be a good thing.

Sata headed towards the rows of trees by camp. Ilika had said a lot, and she had a lot to think about. She knew she had an infatuation for Boro, but would he stay with Josa, or would he say no and let them get closer? The whirlwind of questions flooded her mind until she heard a voice behind her.

"Sata, wait up!"

She turned around quizzically to see Kibi jogging towards her, trying to catch up. She gave a small smile and waited for her friend. "What's up, Kibi?"

"You don't want to wander all alone, that's dangerous. Why are you heading out here anyway?"

Sata looked at her friend shyly. "I was just going for a walk."

"Oh, alright," Kibi said, not buying it. "Want a walking buddy?"

"Sure," the young girl said with a smile.

"Cool, let's go!" Kibi grinned as she linked arms with her friend and headed into the trees.

Sata kept quiet most of the way, letting Kibi talk about the camp and the people, not caring to mention anything about her conversation with Ilika.

"Sata?"

She looked up to see Kibi looking questioningly at her.

"Yeah?"

"You're not listening . . . what are you thinking about?"

"I'm not thinking about anything," Sata said as she and her friend stopped walking and looked eye-to-eye.

"Uh huh, right," she said disapprovingly, putting her hands on her hips. "Come on, Sata, we're friends, aren't we?"

"Of course we are, Kibi."

"Then why aren't you telling me the truth? Friends don't lie to each other." Kibi watched as a sad look came over Sata, so she did what she thought was best and put her arm around the girl. "If you don't want to talk about it, I understand."

Sata remained quiet for a long time, and Kibi stepped back, letting her think. "Ilika and I talked, that's all."

"You and Ilika?" Kibi repeated, raising her eyebrows. "What about?"

"Boro."

Kibi smiled. "About his obvious marriage proposal from the goat lady?"

"Yeah . . . I don't want him to stay, Kibi. I know that's wrong of me, that I should want what Boro wants, but I just can't help it! I like him!" Sata threw her hand over her mouth as her face turned an instant beet-red.

Kibi tried to suppress a laugh. "I know you do."

"How did you know?"

"Sata, you and Boro have been attached to one another since you began talking to each other. You two have been getting closer as people, just as Ilika and I have."

"Yeah . . . what would you do if Ilika had the chance to walk away?"

Kibi looked back towards the camp through the trees and saw Ilika helping the other students, with his seemingly-permanent smile. "I'd want him to be happy. If I'm not what makes him happiest, I don't want him to stay. It'd hurt for him to ever leave . . . I like him just as you like Boro. But at the same time, if you like someone like that, you have to be ready for things to change, for someone to decide that happiness would be better found elsewhere. We all hope that it doesn't happen, but sometimes it does anyway, no matter what we try to do about it."

Sata looked down and thought for a long moment. "I guess you're right."

Kibi touched her sad friend's shoulder. "Boro is a good guy, and will make a good partner someday. But you may learn about him through this. Though I think he'll make the right decision.

Sata smiled gently. "That's what Ilika told me, only a little different."

"Great minds think alike," Kibi said with a shy smile. "I know you understand where we're coming from, too. I think Boro really likes you. I don't think he'd give you up at this point. But if he does, then I know you'll be just fine. You're a strong girl, and no boy can change that."

"I hope so!" Sata said with a grin, which slowly faded after a moment. "I've just been lonely, Kibi. I don't know how I'd keep being happy if Boro wasn't here."

Pretty Kibi looked at her friend with an expression Sata couldn't place. "Sata, if you don't mind me being honest with you, I think that you need to realize something."

"Go ahead," Sata said softly.

"Boro isn't the only thing that can make you happy. You need to be able to make yourself happy before any boy can take on the responsibility. You should be confident and content without Boro there to do it for you. I had to learn that the hard way ... there was a boy once, back when I was a slave, that I thought would make me happier than I could be otherwise. But I had to give him up to another girl, because that's what he decided would make him happiest. That was okay, though, looking back on it now. If he wouldn't have done what makes him happy, then I wouldn't be where I am now with Ilika, I'd still be thinking that only he could make me the person I am. After he left, I had to make the decision to be happy with myself, and to want to be who I am now."

Sata looked down and laced her fingers together, playing with her hands as she listened to her friend's words. "I understand."

"I have to make myself happy. I have to be happy with who I am. Once I did that, I was able to let myself be with Ilika and feel like I do for Ilika. I'm the happiest I've ever been, it all started with me."

"I know what you're saying, Kibi. Before anyone else can make me happy, I need to do it by myself."

"See? You're a quick learner." Kibi smiled.

"It's going to be hard," Sata said slowly, "but with friends like you by my side, I'll be okay no matter what Boro does."

"There you go! I knew you'd be able to do it!" Kibi pulled in her friend and hugged her tightly. "Come on, Sata, let's get back to camp before Ilika gets on both of us for being gone so long!"

"Alright, Kibi ... and thank you, for everything. I'm okay now, and I know I always will be, thanks to what you've done for me today."

Kibi smiled and linked arms with the young girl. "What're friends for?"

✳ ✳ ✳

Boro and Sata

by Terri Snyder

This story takes place during the last few chapters of *NEBADOR Book One: The Test*, and most of *NEBADOR Book Two: Journey.*

Back in the capital city, Boro thought Sata was pretty cute. He couldn't come right out and talk about it like Miko and Neti could, but he was looking and thinking, and liked what he saw.

Everything was pretty easy until they almost got arrested, and then had to creep under a building to get into the city walls. Boro noticed that Sata was a faithful friend to Mati. That made him smile.

It was the pool of cold, dark water under the wall that really made him take a good look at her. She was strong and smart when some people were freaking out. She could swim, and didn't start shivering just because of a little cold water. He liked that.

But he only had time to think about it once they got to the old shack and Mati was trying to ride her new donkey. He watched Mati and Tera, like everyone else, but he was thinking about Sata.

She was strong on the trail to Farmer Keni's place, and then on the hills west of there. Math was a little hard for her, but Boro couldn't complain, because he was worse!

She wasn't afraid of the blood when Shepherdess Noni had to deliver a lamb, and helped him and Miko carry the mother sheep back to the camp. Boro was getting more and more impressed.

Then came a big scare for Boro. At the hot springs, Sata got all religious, and started thinking the place was evil. For a while he thought she was going to go get a priest. He told her to stuff it, and she didn't take it too well. But then Ilika, and everyone else, told her the same thing. He watched her as she swallowed her pride, poked around the hot springs and steam vent by herself for a whole day, and finally got over it.

It was along the ocean when Boro got really curious. Every time Sata came back from the beach, especially when she had been sitting out there alone, it was like she had been talking to an old friend. He knew she had some good talks with Ilika, but the ocean seemed to be telling her things too.

She was nice to Kit, but let Kibi and Buna do most of the talking. That was ok. Boro could tell that the little kid got really antsy when too many people were trying to be nice to him at once.

He noticed Sata was pretty scared when the thieves surrounded them near Port Town, but he didn't worry about it. Almost everyone was scared. Him too, a little.

When she jumped into the water at high tide to help him with the donkey, that's when he knew she was the kind of girl he really liked. There was nothing *really* dangerous about that waterfall bowl. He knew it, and after she jumped in, he could tell that she knew it too.

Miko didn't get it. Boro kind of liked Miko because he was strong in some ways that Boro wasn't, like talking to girls. But Miko was carrying some deep, dark fear that Boro didn't understand. Somehow it made him change the waterfall bowl, which was just a little uncomfortable, into a deadly monster. Boro didn't relate to that, and he could tell Sata didn't either.

It didn't surprise Boro at all that she was strong and did what he said during the fire at Lumber Town. Maybe he wished she had been a little nicer to Toli, but not much nicer. She kept Toli moving so he could figure out which way to go, and that really helped.

All that day, he felt like he had a huge weight on his shoulders, responsible for saving not just himself, but Sata and Toli too. When they found little Tati, the weight became worse. But all during that day, Sata was there at his side, taking as much of the weight as she could. That's what made it possible for Boro to keep going. He was *so* glad when they got to the fishing village.

Boro could really see the frustration Kibi was feeling as she tried to keep everyone's spirits up while they waited for Ilika and his group. He knew he wasn't doing a very good job keeping his own spirits up, and neither was Sata, but he sensed it was a time to go easy on everyone, including himself.

When they walked back through Lumber Town and there were dead bodies everywhere, he kept an eye on Sata again. She used to be a little freaked out about people dying, because she hadn't been a slave. She frowned a lot when they looked at the smoking ruins, but was ok. Boro was glad.

Then they came to Farmer Koto's house, and there was Josa.

She was strong, pretty, skilled in many ways from growing up on a ranch, and ready to get married. She was everything Boro could have wanted. He listened to her bravely tell him all her desires as they walked in the moonlight. All he had to do was say yes.

While Boro walked with Josa, Sata cried with Ilika.

Something kept Boro from saying yes to Josa. It wasn't anything about Josa, and it wasn't anything about Sata. It was *how* he knew Sata that made him say no to Josa. He didn't just know Sata, he had already shared a chunk of his life with her. He had shared his *entire* life as a free grown up with her. He barely remembered being free as a little kid, so that didn't count.

He only shared a walk in the moonlight with Josa. That just didn't compare to working with Sata in the pool under the city wall, and all the other things they had done together.

Even before Boro put his bedroll beside hers, she knew Ilika was right. If Boro didn't stay with her, she didn't want him. It was just hard to admit it to herself.

I know. I am Sata.

* * *

Buna's Search

by Shadow Buffalo-walker

This story takes place after Buna and Misa bid farewell to Ilika and the others near the swamp in *NEBADOR Book Three: Selection*.

Misa and I didn't mind walking to the capital city with Neti and Toli. I knew our paths would go different ways very soon. Neti kept saying things about us all sticking together. I could tell Misa didn't like the idea, and I didn't like it either. My guts told me we should split up right then, but I didn't say anything just to be nice to Neti. Then Toli got all dorky at the city gate and it cost us more to get in because of it. I should have listened to my guts.

By the time we got to the marketplace, I was glad Neti wanted to get a room at the inn before doing anything else. Toli was like a little puppy and did everything she said. Misa and I waved good-bye. When they were gone, we both laughed our heads off and took Tera to a stable. The bakery still had some tarts so we got a bunch and sat down on a log to eat our dinner.

"Boots!" Misa said. "I'm gonna get boots!"

We stayed at the witch's house for three days and Misa got her boots. I'm glad we didn't stay any longer because the religious orders were getting weird. I kept seeing things I could spend my money on, but then I thought about how I had to drag everything around while I looked for Noni. I could either buy stuff, and a wagon, and horses to pull it, or I could look for Noni. I decided to look for Noni.

✳

We visited the old shack and the corral. I think Tera remembered it, but didn't like it when I put her inside and closed the gate. She was glad when we left the next day.

Farmer Keni sold us bread and cheese. Kora remembered me, and said she was happy there and had forgotten all about reading and writing and stuff. While we were there a boy came down the road, and they ran up to the goat pen together. Misa smiled. I think she likes boys.

After that we went into the hills and all the way down to the hot springs. I showed Misa the little camp by the stream, and the sandy place where Noni camped once, but we didn't find Noni anywhere. Misa loved the hot springs, and so did I. She asked if we could stay there forever. A part of me almost wanted to say yes.

We traveled north to Lumber Town, and some other little towns. Misa asked everywhere about her parents, but never found them. Lumber Town had one little store made of new logs and boards, but no inn yet. No one was trying to rebuild her old burned house.

Winter was coming and snow started falling around Lumber Town so we headed south. We visited the house with good people where all the refugees had gone, and they gave us dinner after we carried firewood, but all the people we remembered were gone.

At the little fishing village called Fish, we had fish stew one more time, and camped in the trees, but didn't go onto the beach south of there. I told Misa why it was so dangerous. She shrugged and wanted to go that way, and if we didn't have Tera, I probably would have said ok. I remembered how hard it was to keep Tera under control when she was scared.

On the road south, I saw some sheep for sale by an old shepherd who was gonna live with his son. It was really tempting. I asked if he knew Noni, and he did, but hadn't seen her in months.

When we got to Port Town, I told Misa about all the thieves, and she spotted them as soon as we walked into town. I was glad I hadn't bought any new clothes, and Misa's boots already looked old, so they didn't bother us.

We stayed with the baker all winter. Misa and Kit were like two peas in a pod, and she didn't care that he could hardly talk. He could laugh and play, and that was all that mattered. He showed her his mother's grave. After he curled up to take a nap, I pulled Misa away and showed her the cave by the beach.

I asked all around Port Town if anyone had seen Noni. One sheep shearer remembered her, but hadn't seen her since last spring.

All winter we worked for the baker, and on our days off we walked to little towns and farms and asked about Noni. Sometimes people knew her, but hadn't seen her in a long time.

The next summer we walked all over the kingdom, except the mountains where Noni couldn't go with her wagon and flock. No one in the eastern part of the kingdom knew her, and thought it was weird that a girl would be a shepherdess without a man. One person in the middle of the kingdom remembered her, but hadn't seen her in years.

Even in the western part, people were starting to forget her. I figured out that no one had seen her since about when I first met her. I started to wonder if maybe she was just a spirit that had floated away into the clouds after me and Ilika's other students had said good-bye and gone down to the hot springs. That now seemed a long time ago.

✳

Misa was getting very tired of looking. She kept talking about Port Town, and the baker and his family, and Kit, and the hot springs.

I sighed and felt in my guts that it was time to let go of Noni.

We returned to Port Town, bought a wagon, twelve sheep, and lots of boards and nails. Misa asked Kit if he wanted to join us. He was confused for a while, but said yes when we told him we were gonna stay near Port Town and visit it often.

We took everything up the green valley and built a little house by the hot springs. The sheep loved the grass and started having babies.

I had forgotten all about Noni when one day, in the middle of summer, a shepherd's wagon pulled by a donkey came wobbling along the trail to the hot springs followed by ninety-three sheep.

✳   ✳   ✳

The Magic Needle

by Kathleen Tully

This story depicts the future of Risan Gor after her rescue by the crew of the Manessa Kwi, at Melorania's direction, near the end of *NEBADOR Book Four: Flight Training.*

Timod Gor's gold didn't last long. He drank up some of it, smoked some, bought whores with a lot, gave some away to impress people, and gambled. He was at the card table when he ran out of gold, and thought he had a good hand, so he bet his daughter. He lost the hand, but suddenly sobered up enough to realize what he had done and refused to give her to the winner. The winner didn't like being cheated, a dagger flashed out, and even before Timod Gor hit the floor, little Risan Gor ran out into the black night faster than anyone could follow.

She didn't touch her gold, still hidden on the hill, for a long, long time. It felt dirty because it had made her father stupid with drink and smoke and gambling. So she just walked, and when she saw people on the road, she hid in the bushes until they were close enough to tell if they were good people or bad.

Most of the time, the people were good when she thought they were. She asked if she could work for her food. Sometimes they said yes. Sometimes they were too poor and had to say no. Sometimes they were bad and she had to run again. Luckily she was too young for them to care much about catching.

※

For two years she worked doing anything people wanted her to. Slowly she discovered she was best at sewing, because she had long, nimble fingers, and she liked doing it. So when she came to a new village or farm, she started saying she was a seamstress. Often enough to keep her fed, they needed one.

Risan Gor was eight, and getting really good at sewing, when she started saving up some copper pieces. One day she saw some fancy new iron needles in the marketplace, and the woman said they lasted a lot longer than bone needles. The girl dug into her money pouch and counted out the precious coins.

By the time she was nine, she would arrive in a town and people would start whispering, "It's Risan the Seamstress! Tell the innkeeper! He's got lots of mending to do!" Soon she had copper AND silver pieces in her pouch, and half a dozen iron needles, of different shapes and sizes, in her shoulder bag along with *four* colors of thread. She still kept the bone needles, just to remember her younger days.

The years passed, and Risan the Seamstress liked to go on walks in the woods when she wasn't sewing. She was eleven when she found a pretty, shiny rock, so she put it into her bag. Back in her tiny one-room workshop, the shiny rock was sitting on the work table when she happened to toss an iron needle near it. The needle jumped, and stuck to the rock!

She nearly ran to the blacksmith.

"Sir, what kind of rock is this? My iron sewing needles stick to it!"

"Hmm. I've heard of these. Some kind of strange iron that fell from the sky, some say. I can't think of any use for it." He tossed the rock back to her.

She couldn't think of any use for it either, so she just used it on her work table to hold her needles.

Risan was twelve when she happened to drop her smallest iron needle, the one she used for embroidery, into a cup of water. The needle floated on the surface of the water, and quickly pointed toward the shiny rock, only about a foot away. She looked at it for a minute, then dried it off and went back to sewing.

About a month later, she set down her smallest needle after some embroidery work that left her fingers sore, and was about to take a drink of water. She looked at the needle and the cup of water, and remembered the first time. But this time was different. She had taken the shiny rock to show a friend, and had accidentally left it there. *What would the needle do*, she wondered, *without the rock near? Would it point toward her friend's house?*

She carefully dropped the needle into the water, and it floated, just like the first time. It started slowly swinging to point at something, but it wasn't her friend's house. She stepped outside to make sure. Yep, she was right — her friend's house was a different direction.

This new thing she had discovered was funny, but she couldn't think of any use for it, so she went back to sewing.

Risan the Seamstress started dreaming about whatever the needle was pointing to when the shiny rock wasn't near. She could never quite see it, so far away and shrouded in mist in the dream. But she woke up curious.

Her twelfth year was passing into her thirteenth when she could stand it no longer. She was, honestly, getting tired of dreaming about pointing needles. A dream about a handsome young man, now and then, would be nice.

She started putting a small wooden cup and her embroidery needle into her shoulder bag whenever she went walking. At the town well, just a block from her house, she got a cup of water, found a place to sit where no one could see, and put the needle in. It pointed straight back to her workshop, where the rock sat on the table.

But at the stream outside of town, it slowly went a different way again. At the river two miles away, it did the same thing. At three other places, all a mile or more away from the village, the needle pointed to . . .

"Sir," she asked an old man pulling his little boat onto the riverbank, "are you a sailor?"

"Was when I was young and strong. Sailed the five seas for twenty years."

"So you know how to tell directions?"

"Sure do! On most ships, I was the closest thing they had to a navigator."

"Can you tell me what direction it is to that mountain that looks like a bird's beak?"

"Buzzard's Peak, that's called. Every sailor 'round here knows *that* direction, 'cause it's right under the North Star, the star that all the Heavens rotate around. That's *north*, little lady, about as perfect as anyone can tell."

✳

Risan the Seamstress was fourteen when she started remembering something that had happened to her at age five. She remembered a journey by ship, then bad weather, and finally a very cold place with ice in every direction, even floating on the sea.

For some reason, the way she and her father had been rescued was hard to remember. She didn't *want* to remember what came next — her father drinking and smoking and gambling, then getting killed and leaving her alone. But her mind kept wandering back to the voyage by ship, and she started remembering voices.

"What do you *mean* you don't know which direction to go?" the captain bellowed.

"I haven't been able to see the stars for days!" the frightened man whined. "North could be that way, or that way, or . . ."

The conversation ended when the captain thrust a dagger between the navigator's ribs.

Risan brought her mind back to the present, ripped out a couple of stitches she had gotten in the wrong place because of daydreaming, and mumbled to herself, "He must not have had a magic needle. He must not have even *known* about magic needles."

In the days that followed, she started to wonder if maybe that strange rock of hers had a use after all.

She was fifteen when she realized several things at about the same time, and thinking about them nearly made her sick. She wasn't pretty enough to catch the eye of any of the handsome young men. She didn't know how to do anything but sew. And her hands were becoming stiff and sore, more and more quickly, while she worked. It the stiffness kept getting worse, in just a few years she'd be unable to sew enough to pay the rent and buy food.

A month later, she quit taking new sewing jobs, finished the ones she was working on, packed a bag, and walked out the door before paying the rent that was due. She took her strange, shiny rock, a few small iron needles, one spool of thread, and a wooden cup, but little else. She was not planning to set up a new sewing business somewhere else. She was casting herself into the wind to see what the world would show her.

After a week of travel, she was wandering along the docks of the port city of her kingdom. At first she was lost in her thoughts, but slowly started to realize that something was wrong. There were four great sailing ships in the harbor, but no cargos were being loaded or unloaded. Each had a man or two standing guard, but nothing else was happening. She became curious and approached one of the ships.

"Hey there, sailor! What news from the sea?"

"You watch your tongue, young woman, for I be not some lousy sailor, but am truly the *captain* of this proud vessel . . . for all the good it does me."

"Why would a captain speak in such tones? Is she not a fair ship that races before the wind?"

"She would be, if she had any work to do. Now . . . she just rots in the harbor, and neither she, nor I, like it much."

Risan the ex-seamstress got comfortable on a crate at the edge of the wharf. "What keeps her from having work, if I may ask. I am without work right now out of choice, but not you, I take it."

"Certainly not! I'd be hauling cargos back and forth across the sea if anyone dared send them anymore. It's in my blood. I can do nothing else. If I cannot sail, I might as well lie down and die."

"Why do they not send cargos?"

"Too many ships lost. Too much bad weather. Hardly half get to the far shore. Some, they say, end up at the bottom of the world where there is nothing but ice. Most are never seen again. One made it back from there, a few years ago, and told of the bones of ships scattered on the ice and the bones of men piled on the shore."

Risan swallowed. "I've been there," she said softly.

"Have ye? Well, you're one of the few who can say that and still draw breath to boast of it."

She was thoughtful for a while. "What would be your chances of getting across the sea safely if you had something . . . something magical . . . that always pointed north?"

His eyes grew very large. "My stars, I'd be the luckiest captain in the kingdom! I'd be able to guide the helmsman true even in the worst storm or fog! But such a magical thing does not exist, does it?"

"It does, and I have one."

"Well, you come right aboard, young woman, and I shall make you . . . you don't mind soup and bread, do you?"

"I love soup and bread. I was a seamstress, nothing fancy."

They talked for hours, ate soup and bread, drank ale, and became friends. But the captain still frowned whenever the talk circled around to his ship once again carrying cargos.

"What bothers you?" Risan asked.

"It takes more than a ship and a magical north-finder. It takes a patron."

"What's that?"

"An investor, a rich man who *believes* the voyage will be successful, believes it enough to put up the four or five great gold pieces for a crew, supplies, and a cargo to sell on the far shore. After so many ships lost, there's hardly a patron to be found. And believe me, Risan, me saying I know a young woman with a magical north-finder, an unproven gadget no one's ever heard of, is not going to shake even a *copper* piece out of anyone's money pouch, much less the gold that would be needed. So unless *you* know of a patron who would take such a risk . . ."

Her mind went back ten years and struggled to remember something . . . something about gold . . . gold that her father didn't know about. She glimpsed, in her memory, a shaggy black-haired . . . lady? . . . angel? . . . burying something . . . a metal tube with something very heavy inside. She saw the log the angel-lady put over the hiding place. She saw the hill it was on from the road to the village.

"How far is it from here to Tolek?" she asked the captain.

"That little sheep and cattle village in the hills? Half a day on a horse, or a long day's walk."

"I think I know . . . a patron there who . . . would believe in my north-finder. What does a patron get for his risk?"

"If the voyage is successful, he gets his money back and *at least* another great gold, sometimes two, depending on how well the cargo sells. And with so few ships making it, I *know* the cities across the sea will pay good money for our wares."

Risan Gor ate her soup and bread silently for a little while longer.

"I'm going on a little journey. If I find . . . the patron . . . I'll be back in . . . two or three days with five great gold pieces. Will you be here?"

He grinned, pulled her close, and kissed her.

Note from J. Z. Colby: It is true that the compass was already in use in the kingdom that is the setting of *NEBADOR Books One*, *Two*, and *Three*, but this story takes place in a different kingdom. It is often the case in history that inventions come to one part of a world before, sometimes long before, another. Even more strange are those moments in history when discoveries are made at multiple locations at about the same time, but without any cross-influence.

*　*　*　*　*

Part 4

This part recounts the story of the inhabitants of one area of Sonmatia Four about 20,000 years earlier, from *NEBADOR Book Five: Back to the Stars.*

The Monuments of Zolko

King Zolko struggled to pull enough air into his lungs as he sat on his throne and looked over the shriveled fruit and hard bread on the silver platter close at hand. For a moment he bristled, then relaxed as he remembered the even-poorer food in the marketplace these days. Several councilors sat in lesser chairs, also struggling to breathe while keeping their gaze respectfully low.   Servants stood, hands behind their backs, trying to hide their discomfort.

The great doors at the far end of the hall opened, and a well-dressed man strode in.   For a moment, harsh sunlight entered, along with some reddish-brown dust. The door guards quickly closed the doors and tried to muffle their coughing.

"Councilor Ganlo!" the king said with both a friendly greeting and frustration. "Why is the air so thin today? Did you speak to the priests and scholars?"

Ganlo stopped the proper distance from the throne and bowed. "I did, Your Majesty, as many as I could find. Some have abandoned their duties and left the city. The priests have been praying day and night, they say, and the scholars have searched every book. No one knows what else can be done to appease the gods."

The king suddenly stood, his chin thrust forward. "The scholars have repeatedly stood before me and proclaimed that all important knowledge is in their books! I want all of you on the streets, searching for answers! I will not let this be the end of our great kingdom!"

The other councilors, most of them old men, started to rise.

"Sire, there is one other possibility," Ganlo said, head half-bowed.

"Speak!"

"There is a woman in the marketplace. She calls herself a prophet, but the priests deny it. She says we need not fear, that the gods will save our kingdom by taking a few to a new land flowing with nut milk and honey. She gathers people around her to listen, and children sit in her lap and are comforted."

The king stood thoughtfully, rubbing his chin. "How does she say the chosen few will be selected?"

"I do not know, Sire."

"Go! All of you! Sit at her feet and listen, and come back in three days with what you learn!"

✳

The councilors of King Zolko listened to the prophet for two days, and when she was at table eating, or asleep, they questioned the priests and scholars further. Some of the councilors became convinced that the wrath of the gods could be appeased by great works. Others were not so optimistic, and tried to discover how the chosen few would be selected, as the king had ordered.

On the third day, Councilor Sarto crept away and sold all his property to hire a ship and many strong men. He believed the gods would look favorably on them if they found the most beautiful gemstone in the world and placed it in the temple. He carried books and maps from the great library, all telling him that such a gemstone could only be found across the sea, in the Desert of Bakka, somewhere along the eight degree line, for that was the number most sacred to the gods.

Also on the third day, Councilor Memna, the greatest politician in the kingdom and the king's official speaker, slipped away from the group to sell all her property and hire a ship. "I shall create a city in the wilderness, seventy-six kilometers west by northwest of here. All who love the gods may come, bring their children, and help make a society of peace and harmony. The gods will see our creation of love, smile upon us, and make the wind to blow and the rain to fall."

Word spread rapidly, and when she arrived at the dock to board the ship, hundreds of people were already assembled and ready to follow, in rowboats if necessary.

✳

On the evening of the third day, Ganlo and the few other remaining councilors entered the king's hall.

"Your Majesty, we are divided on how the gods might be appeased. Sarto seeks the most beautiful gemstone. Memna plans to create a city of peace and harmony. The priests, however, are convinced that only great monuments would be pleasing to the gods, monuments bearing the likeness of the high kings, such as yourself, and the high priests . . ."

"But I sent you to learn how the chosen few will be selected!"

"We were able to discover little, Sire. The prophet only babbles about children and their pure hearts. I don't think she knows."

The king questioned the other councilors. They were all in agreement with Ganlo, and could add little else. Silence prevailed in the great hall as the king rubbed his chin. Finally, he spoke. "So be it. Scribes!"

Two old men emerged from nearby rooms and sat down at writing desks.

"Let it be known that all men, and all women not with child, must report to the palace at sunrise every morning until suitable monuments have been raised to let the gods see the faces of all the high kings and high priests of the land."

"But Sire," Ganlo interrupted, "bringing that much stone from beyond the sea will take years."

The king took a breath of the thin air. "Then we shall not use new stone. We shall take down the buildings of the city, one by one. If necessary, only the foundation of the palace will be spared, a place for the gods to rest as they admire the beauty and grandeur of the Monuments of Zolko!"

✳   ✳   ✳

The City of Memna

Councilor Memna worked side by side with her people, never asking them to do anything she wasn't willing to do. So it was that they worked with glad hearts, and within a year they all had houses and the new city was functioning well.

The air seemed to get no worse, and some even said it was a little better. The drought continued and the crops were poor, but they shared alike in what they had, and Memna made sure no one hoarded more than their share of anything. She dispensed justice as cases were brought to her, barely pausing in her work with stone chisel or garden hoe in hand. The people around her listened to her wise words as they worked, and knew in their hearts they had chosen the right path and their city would be pleasing to the gods.

"Why do you not take the best food and live a life of leisure, like King Zolko?" a young woman asked, pausing in her work to comfort her baby.

Memna smiled. "The gods are pleased when each citizen gives what she is able, and only takes what she needs. That is the essence of civilized life. King Zolko's way is the way of the animals in the jungle of Torku."

The girl smiled and returned to her work.

✳

As the months of the second year began to pass, some of the people of the City of Memna became unhappy. Memna's judgments always favored social harmony, and whenever that goal was in conflict with the needs of an individual, the group won and the person lost.

Those who saw the city as a hive, whose purpose was to function as efficiently as possible, were happy. Artists and other sorts of free-thinkers did not feel the same.

Also, travelers occasionally arrived from the old capital city, now being quickly dismantled to create the monuments King Zolko had ordered. They hoped to find better air, less dust, and perhaps a little rain, but were disappointed. Memna tried to silence them and brand them as heretics, but the truth crept throughout the city like a disease.

Some people gathered in houses late in the evenings to carry on the traditions of their previous guilds and orders. One such order contained a couple of old masters and several young students, all dedicated to mental discipline and psychic abilities. After doing her share of the work of the city for more than a year and a half, Nosta, a young woman of the order, decided it was time to act. She knelt before her masters one evening.

"I believe the City of Memna is pleasing to many of the people, those who never have an original thought in their heads. I do not believe the gods are so small-minded. I have repaired a little boat that no one wanted, and I plan to depart tonight. I will find the fabled Arch on the Island of Glimpa, where I will sit in meditation until the gods receive my offering of mind and spirit, or until I die."

*

The masters and the other students of the order quickly gathered as much bread and dried fruit as they could find, and went down to the shore to see their brave friend off in the darkness. Nosta was never seen again by mortal eyes.

After that time, the air became thinner and thinner, and no more clouds appeared in the yellowing sky. The crops failed at both the Monuments of Zolko and the City of Memna. By the end of the second year, the people were dying and had forgotten all about the joys of peace and harmony. No one in either city claimed to know what might be pleasing to the gods.

*   *   *

The Fabled Arch of Glimpa

Day one. I rowed all night long. As the sun rose, my arms felt like lead, but I dared not stop or I would drift south. I entered a second-level walking meditation, but willed my arms to move instead of my feet. In a clear sky, the sun seemed bent on cooking me. Somehow, as the blessed evening finally arrived, I crawled onto the rocks at the south end of Glimpa.

Day four. The sun-blisters on my hands and arms are beginning to harden. The air is so thin, I drag myself along slowly, ever searching for the Arch. I found one spring with water, but many others are dry.

Day seven. The fabled Arch stretches itself before me, silent as a . . . tomb. My tomb, I guess. Whether the gods accept my humble gift or not, I know my mortal body is done. I shall never know the touch of a mate, nor bear a child. Perhaps, if my offering is accepted, the wind will blow again, the rain will fall, and my friend Kelsa will ask Regno to join with her, and they will have a daughter and name her Nosta.

Day eleven. At sunrise I sit on the Arch to salute the new day and summon courage and joy into my heart where dread and fear lurk in waiting. I can see smoke rising from the City of Memna, and in the exact opposite direction, somewhere in the Desert of Bakka, more smoke from the Mines of Sarto. By mid-morning I seek the shade beneath the Arch, and descend into the deepest levels of meditation. Slowly, without any act of will, I allow my spirit to rise up to Heaven.

Day fifteen. I am completely out of food. I am too weak to travel far, and the only things growing here are bitter and make me lose more than they give me. Even if I had the will to return to the boat, I know I would die on the way. No, I will finish what I started, here, at Glimpa's Arch. The act belongs to me, the consequence, pleasing or not, belongs to the gods.

Day seventeen. I can no longer climb the Arch to see the sunrise. My world has shrunk to the little strip of shade beneath the Arch as it moves from hour to hour.

Day twenty-one. Yesterday I sat in the most joyful awareness of the gods for half the day and all the night. The morning glow in the sky was like a gift to me, a little private celebration, for I no longer have the strength to follow the shade. After I write this, I will prop myself against the base of my beloved Arch, giving everything in my mind and heart and spirit to the gods. As the sun climbs into the sky, I will die.

My hand shakes and I can write no more.

✳ ✳ ✳

The Mines of Sarto

No writings or recordings have been discovered that detail the lives of the people who worked these mines. Apparently all of the people who labored here were driven by an intense desire to find a gemstone worthy of offering to their gods. There is no evidence of slavery.

Nor were there any class or status differences. Councilor Sarto appears to have worked right alongside the other miners, day after day, until the very end. Judging by the positions of bodies, tools, and gemstones, the following reconstruction of events seems most likely:

Sarto and his followers decided on this location about half a year after crossing the sea. With shovels and blasting powder, they dug shafts into the bedrock until they found veins of crystals that angled deep into the planet. These they followed as far as they could, bringing every find to the surface to be cleaned and inspected.

About a year into their work, they could go no deeper as carbon dioxide began to fill the lower tunnels. Many miners died from the bad air or sheer exhaustion. Sarto and a few hearty followers pressed on, taking turns working for just a few minutes each in the deep places.

Those who could no longer work in the mines helped to clean and sort the crystals, each hoping to find the object of their quest. When nothing else could be done, they burned whatever they could find to send their prayers up to the gods.

The day came when only Sarto and one other miner remained alive. The miner was large and strong, but his name is not known. He struggled up from one of the deep tunnels, placed a dirt-filled box at Sarto's feet, and died.

After honoring the fallen man with tools in his hands and gemstones over his eyes, Sarto was amazed to find, in the box of dirt, the most beautiful cluster of crystals he had ever seen. Alone, he lovingly cleaned the precious object. With his last bit of strength, Sarto placed it on a boulder for the gods to see, cried himself to sleep, and never woke up.

※　※　※　※　※

Part 5

The following short story is the Third Place winner of the Last NEBADOR Writing Contest, 2014-2016.

The Lonely Space Dragon

by Sammy McNeil

This story takes place primarily in the region of the broken planet Sonmatia Five, which we call an asteroid belt. The crew of the Manessa Kwi visited one piece of it, planetary fragment five-three-three, in *NEBADOR Book Five: Back to the Stars.*

The space dragon was playing with his friends on a nice sunny day. Every day is sunny in space, so he and his friends played every day. Whack-An-Asteroid was their favorite game, but sometimes they played Hide-And-Seek in the rings and moons of one of the gas giant planets.

Everything changed so fast, the space dragon's head was still spinning hours later. Something had exploded, and all the space dragons went tumbling for millions of miles.

When he finally quit tumbling, none of his friends were around, the planets and asteroids and comets all looked different, and even the sun was a different color. He was lost and alone.

*

At first, the space dragon felt afraid. But slowly it came to him that he never had to clean up his asteroids ever again, and he never had to mop or dust the planets where he had made a mess. He started to think that maybe being alone wasn't so bad.

He explored his new home. It had four rocky planets, another one that had broken up into asteroids, four gas giants, and some moons and comets and other small things. One of the planets had some little tiny creatures on it, and another had some tiny crumbling buildings, but not another space dragon anywhere.

The space dragon started to feel lonely.

*

After taking a nap, the space dragon decided to look for a friend. Maybe there were no other space dragons, but maybe there was someone who would be his friend.

He started with the asteroid belt where he felt most at home. Some of the pieces were big enough to have caves, so he looked into all of them, and called out, "Is anyone in there? I'm looking for a friend."

There were some pretty crystals in some of the caves, but no one the space dragon could play with.

Next he spotted a comet flying toward the sun. He knew that comets sometimes had giant ice spiders. They were a bit serious, and didn't like to play Whack-An-Asteroid, but maybe one of them would be his friend.

He flew all around the comet, dodging chunks of rock and ice that broke off to make the tail. "Any giant ice spiders want to play?" he called.

After a while he gave up. This comet didn't have any giant ice spiders, or anyone else.

He tried all the planets. The first one didn't have anything but tiny crystals almost too small to see. The second was all yellow air and crumbled building, and no one alive that he could see. The third had lots of little animals, but they all acted afraid of the space dragon and hid in their houses, caves, or trees. And anyway, few of them could fly in the air, and none of them could fly in space, so they were boring.

The fourth planet didn't have much air, which was fine with the space dragon, but no one was alive. Only a few old stones showed the space dragon that maybe someone had lived there once, a long time ago.

The space dragon sighed, and took another nap in the sunshine.

*

Soon the space dragon was feeling very sad and bored, so he started playing Whack-An-Asteroid by himself. At first he would play both sides, first whacking, then rushing over to the other side to whack the asteroid back.

That got boring, so he just started whacking at asteroids, not really caring where they went. That helped with his frustration, too.

He had whacked almost a hundred asteroids, but had lost count, when he came to an asteroid that looked different from all the rest. It was a perfect golden ball. He took a good look at it. "Are you an asteroid?" he asked.

The golden ball was silent, so he got ready to give it a good whack with his tail. He was thinking that it might bounce off other asteroids without breaking like the others did. He sung his tail toward it, but hit nothing, and that made him tumble a ways.

After he quit tumbling, he looked back at the golden ball. It had moved! It had moved out of the way when he tried to whack it. That was very strange.

The space dragon flew back and got ready the whack it again. This time he swung his tail slowly so he could keep an eye on the golden ball. His tail moved toward it, but it dashed out of the way again. He didn't tumble this time, since he had flicked his tail slowly.

"You are a very strange asteroid!" he said, not really expecting anyone to hear him. He swung his tail back to take another shot at the golden ball.

"Stop that!" someone said.

The space dragon was so surprised that he quit trying to whack the golden ball. "Who said that?"

The golden ball bounced back and forth a few times. "I did. I'm a very strange asteroid because I'm NOT an asteroid. I'm a ship!"

"What's a . . . ship?" the space dragon asked.

"I'm a container for other being who need to travel a long ways, like . . . maybe . . . a space dragon who has lost his family and friends."

The space dragon just floated in space and frowned.

"Sorry I didn't talk to you sooner, but I had to hear you say a few things to figure out what language you were speaking. Then I had to call my home to find out why you were all alone out here and just whacking asteroids to get out your frustrations."

The space dragon quit frowning since the golden ball seemed to understand him, and that felt nice. "I guess . . . I am . . . frustrated. Sorry I was trying to whack you."

"You're forgiven. So . . . do you want a ride?"

"Um . . . where?"

"Your sun brew up. Space dragons are spread all over the galaxy. Most of them are alone, and none of them like it much. We found them a solar system with lots of asteroids, and no other people that would hate space dragons whacking rocks all over the place. Do you want to join them?"

"Yeah!"

"I have to tell you some things first that you might not like."

The space dragon coiled up and didn't say anything for a long time. The golden ball waited.

Finally the space dragon swallowed. "I don't like hearing bad things."

"I know you don't. You've very young. But I either have to tell you now, or you'll find out when you get there."

"Um . . . okay."

"Not all your family and friends will be there when you arrive. Some died when your sun exploded. Some might be so lost that we'll never find them."

The space dragon felt like crying but didn't want the golden ball to see. "Go away!"

The ship moved away and landed on the far side of the nearest asteroid, but did it slowly enough so the space dragon could see exactly where it went.

✴

An hour later, the space dragon flew slowly around the nearest asteroid. "I . . . want to . . . talk to you some more."

"Okay," the ship said and took off from the asteroid.

"I'd like to have friends to play with again, but I'd rather fly there myself. Will you tell me where they are?"

"Sure, but it would take you about ten years to fly there by yourself, and most of that time you'd be in the darkness between stars. You only got here quickly because of your exploding sun."

"Wow . . . ten years . . . that's a long time."

The golden ball didn't say anything.

"And . . . you can take me there quicker?"

"Yes. It'll take about an hour, and you'll sleep most of the way."

"I like taking naps."

The ship didn't say anything, but opened its hatch and made it big enough for the space dragon.

"Um . . . this is kinda scary. What's in there?"

"Six little animals who help me with everything I need to do. They've cleared the middle of the ship for you, and are in space suits right now because they can't live without air, and the hatch is open."

"Are they . . . nice?"

"Yes, but they can't speak your language, so they'll just run the ship and leave you alone."

The space dragon looked into the hatch. He could see a place big enough for him to coil up in, and he could see the little animals in space suits working at their stations on one side. It looked safe enough. He stuck one toe in. Nothing happened. He stuck his head in. One of the animals waved and then went back to whatever it was doing.

After thinking about it for a little while longer, the space dragon slipped inside the golden ball ship, coiled up in the open space, and soon felt so sleepy, he couldn't keep his eyes open.

✳ ✳ ✳ ✳ ✳

Part 6

The following short story is the Second Place winner of the Last NEBADOR Writing Contest, 2014-2016.

Floating Away

by Tiffany Pertranovich

This story takes place on the gas-giant planet Sonmatia Six, which the crew of the Manessa Kwi saw, but did not visit, in *NEBADOR Book Five: Back to the Stars*.

The green mist was floating at the top of the clouds, looking up at the stars, when a blue mist floated near.

"Hi," the green mist said. "You get done with chores, too?"

"No," the blue mist said. "I snuck away."

The green mist giggled.

"What are you doing up here?" Blue asked.

"Dreaming about the stars. I want to go there some day. I am *so* tired of gravity. Gravity is for *grown-ups!*"

"I know what you mean. Whenever I want to sneak away, I just float up . . . and up . . . and up . . . and no one knows *where* I went!"

Green giggled again. "Want to be friends?"

Blue looked at Green. "And float away together if we can ever find a way?"

Green nodded.

They touched, swirled together, and became a blue-green mist at the top of the clouds.

*

"Assembly!" the evil queen roared. "Everybody get down here, at the bottom of the gravity well where everything is as it should be!" And then she whispered to herself, "(and I'm in control)."

All of the mist-people of Sonmatia Six trudged through the strong gravity to get to the assembly hall. The kids floated, until their parents saw them and made them come down and trudge with the grown-ups.

"Our scientists (damn them) have discovered something!" the evil queen roared when everyone was assembled.

The people gasped, because their queen rarely admitted the scientists even existed, and almost never told the people anything they discovered.

"They have discovered that a comet is coming our way. I didn't believe them until I agreed to look through one of their gadgets. Now I know it's true (and I'm only telling you because I can twist the truth for my own purposes)."

The grown-ups grumbled among themselves. The kids tried to float away, but the grown-ups saw them and made them come back down.

"The comet won't hit the planet, but will skim through the upper cloud layers, and spread poisonous ice made of *water*, and poisonous gasses like *air* . . ."

The people gasped and trembled with fear. The kids tried to float away again, and the grown-ups were so busy trembling that some of the kids made it.

"So even though I hate to do this (but secretly love it)," the evil queen went on, "I have to warn everyone to stay far away from the comet when it skims by, or you might get *poisoned* and *die!*"

The people talked and grumbled and trembled as they left the assembly.

The real truth spread from kid to kid, because one of them had a father who was a scientist, and had heard him saying that the water and air from the comet wasn't poisonous at all.

✳

The next time Green and Blue could get away from chores and lessons, they floated together at the top of the clouds, partly green, partly blue, and partly blue-green.

"I think I can see the comet," Blue said. "If it moves after a while, then that's it, for sure."

"Yeah," Green agreed. "The big question is . . . are we going to do it?"

Blue thought for a long time. "It's a one-way trip. As far as the scientists know, that comet will never come back here . . . even again."

Green nodded. "And we'll have to sneak away three days before it gets here to be at the right place at the right time."

Blue cringed. "Kids our age don't leave home very often, except a few that have rotten parents."

Green nodded. "My parents aren't rotten. They're just . . . grown-ups, and don't understand why I want to go see the . . . the whole . . . the whole universe."

"Mine aren't rotten either," Blue said. "They're just . . . you know . . . caught by gravity."

The two friend were silent for a long time.

"Yep, it moved," Blue said. "That's the comet."

"Yep," Green agreed.

✳

The parents of both Green and Blue arranged plenty of activities, deep in the gravity well, to keep their kids busy on the day the comet would skim the atmosphere of the planet. They had even rented part of Bouncing Cloud Castle, a treat few kids could resist. But they hadn't realized that the most important day for keeping their kids busy was three days earlier.

After a normal day of lessons and chores, the two friends met in a secret place deep inside a dark cloud where no one ever went. They weren't planning to gaze up at the stars and the comet. They were planning to leave home, probably forever.

It was their turn to tremble. Either one of them, alone, probably wouldn't have found the courage to do it. But together, they did.

Without saying much, they took some deep breaths, looked down at their childhood home one last time, and zoomed away toward the place where the comet would skim the clouds of Sonmatia Six three days later.

*

Beings of mist can't zoom very fast. Also, the evil queen's police had thought of what might happen three days before the comet arrived.

"You two kids! Stop right there!"

Green froze, but Blue knew what had to be done. "You go ahead. The police aren't close enough yet to see our colors. I'll puff up real big, and they'll think I'm two of us. Go! Now! Before they get any closer! It was your dream to see the whole universe more than it was mine. And I bet you'll find a way to come back and tell me all about it."

Green hesitated, but Blue gave a big push, and Green knew Blue was being serious. "Bye! I'll never forget you!" Green called, zooming into a cloud.

Blue waved good-bye as long as possible, then puffed up and turned to face the police.

"These must be the missing two kids," one police-mist said.

"We just wanted to see the comet fly by!" Blue said. Then, in a slightly different voice, "Yeah!" Blue agreed, trying not to snicker.

The police took Blue, still puffed up, slowly back down into the gravity well where all the other mist-people lived. They didn't notice that the blue mist had a hint of green in it.

*

Green was sad, but didn't want Blue's sacrifice to be for nothing, so went on, as fast as a mist can, toward the place the comet would touch the clouds.

For two and a half more days, Green floated as fast as possible, not wanting to be late.

When Green arrive at the right place, the comet was almost there. It now looked huge, and Green felt some fear, but Blue's courage had made Green even more determined than ever.

The comet skimmed through the upper clouds, and with a deep breath, Green swirled into the comet's gasses and bits of ice, leaving Sonmatia Six behind forever.

The comet left the clouds and flew back into space.

"Weeeeeeeeeeeee!" Green yelled, starting the biggest adventure any mist-person had ever had.

When the scientists looked through their gadgets at the comet, now getting farther and farther away, they saw a small swirl of green mist among all the white and gray of the comet. They also noticed that the green mist had a little bit of blue in it.

✳ ✳ ✳ ✳ ✳

Farewell to Nebador

In this still moment, after reading about the courage of two friends, Green and Blue, it is time to say good-bye to Nebador.

Ilika, Kibi, Mati, Rini, Boro, Sata, and sometimes Ashley and her team, are out there in the stars, flying their beloved deep-space response ship on missions of all kinds. Susan and Alex have glimpsed Nebador, but have returned home. Daphne, Dem, Tir, and Green have just begun their adventures.

Kodi, Buna, Misa, Toli, Neti, Risan Gor, Liberty, Shawn, Blue, and countless others continue to live their lives on the mortal spheres of time and space, looking for what happiness and purpose they can find.

Miko, Nosta, T'shlix, Jenny, Jimox, Teina, and that girl of many names whom I usually just call Heather, have graduated into the mysteries that lie beyond mortal life.

Kerloran, Melorania, Shemultavia, and Dorolora, who are known by many names, along with others like them who did not enter our story, continue to watch over Nebador.

This humble author, and his readers, are now living close to the times that Heather foresaw, but without the benefit of wise leaders like Susan and Alex. We must, therefore, turn our attention to the years ahead, when the sounds of chugging and whirring cease, and the wild creatures who remain can once again hear each other's voices in life and graceful death.

A few of us might find a place in that world for a little while longer, as witnesses, and for training. Perhaps I will meet you deep in the woods around Mt. Brynion, or somewhere on the banks of the Coweeman River. When the coyotes perk up their ears, listen for the soft sounds of a minor pentatonic flute.

Be well!
J. Z. Colby
2016

About the Cover Artist and Authors

Sidney Oster, the cover artist for *NEBADOR Book Ten*, is a junior in high school where she take several art classes in both two- and three-dimensional art. She has always done art in some capacity. For the past several years, she has enjoyed reading and critiquing the Nebador series, and so it was an honor to do the cover art for *Book Ten*. Outside of school, she really enjoys dancing, mostly tap and lyrical dance. She is also part of her high school robotics team, as she is really interested in the mechanical aspect of building and machining different robot pieces. In addition to dance and robotics, she also shows dogs in AKC conformation shows. In her scarce free time, she likes to cook, read, swim, and spend time with her family.

Mary Anne Brenner, the author of *Still Voices*, is 12 and lives in Australia. She is convinced she learns more from the NEBADOR books than she does in school. She likes to take life slowly, learning and doing everything well, and is very happy, but thinks she might have been even happier one or two centuries ago.

J. Z. Colby, the author of *Escape from Sonmatia Two* and the rest of the NEBADOR series, was born in the Mojave Desert, but now lives and writes deep in a forest of the Pacific Northwest.

He has studied many subjects, formally and informally, including psychology, philosophy, education, and performing arts, but remains a generalist. His primary profession as a mental health counselor, specializing with families and young adults, gives him many stories of personal growth, and the motivation to develop his team of young critiquers and readers.

All his life, he has been drawn toward a broad understanding of human nature, especially those physical, emotional, mental, and spiritual situations in which our capacity to function seems to reach its limits. He finds fascinating those few individuals who can transcend the limits of our common human nature and the dictates of our cultures.

In his spare time, he flies helicopters and airplanes.

He may be contacted at the email address listed on the internet site www.nebador.com.

*

Terri Snyder, the author of *Rini and the Old Slave* and *Boro and Sata*, is 14 and lives in Nevada. She is a serious person who wants to know about all things, especially math and science, even though that doesn't make her popular. In fact, she avoids social networking because it promises friendship but doesn't deliver. Neither does she have any plans of becoming a vampire-lover, but instead likes the simple and honorable donkeys that live in her area.

*

Katelynn Persons, the author of *Kibi and the Search for Happiness, First Taste of Freedom,* and *What're Friends For?* was born and raised in Portland, Oregon until the age of fifteen. She now lives and goes to school in Sandy, Oregon, where she continues her journey through her teenage years. Although she is only seventeen, Katelynn finds much enjoyment in her passions for writing and theater, and was a voice actor and director for the NEBADOR audiobooks.

*

Karen Buchanan, the author of *Buna's New World* and *Neti's Temptation*, is 15 and a native of Quebec, Canada. She speaks both English and French fluently, is learning Spanish, and wants to learn German and Chinese someday. But she has discovered, in the last year, that there are much more important things in life, and is considering literature or art history at university.

*

Chenice Louise Clarke, the author of *Sata's Strength*, is an avid reader, passionate women's rights advocate, and is partial to a cold Coca-Cola or a bar of chocolate. A recent university literature graduate, she loves the theatre, collecting quotes, and spending time with family and friends.

Shadow Buffalo-walker, the author of *Buna's Search*, is completely comfortable on a moon-lit night with coyotes yapping, wolves howling, and buffalo stomping, but has little use for cities and other man-made things. She learned more at the feet of an old native-American woman than in school, but admits that schools are probably necessary for those who want to fit into the human world. For her, it's too late — she has seen the other side, and will spend her life with at least one foot there.

Kathleen Tully, the author of *The Magic Needle*, is 16, lives in Iowa, and loves inventions and discoveries of all kinds. She was identified as highly gifted years ago, is studying every kind of science she can get her hands on in high school, and is preparing to apply to colleges.

Sammy McNeil, the author of *The Lonely Space Dragon*, lives in Cornwall where he and his friends sometimes still make solar systems out of rocks and tree stumps, then lie in the grass and look up at the stars as evening descends over the hills.

Tiffany Pertranovich, the author of *Floating Away*, is a native of New York, where she is anxiously awaiting her 16th birthday, at which time she plans to begin earning her own money and making as many of her own decisions as possible. If she ever becomes a parent (which she seriously doubts), she plans to raise her children wisely so they don't feel weighted down, and are able to grow up as soon as they are ready. She deeply appreciates her own parents for allowing her that freedom.

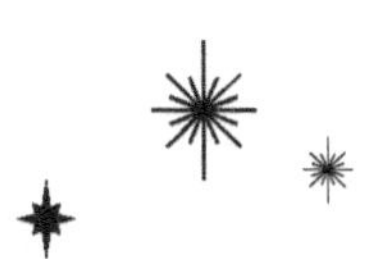